He figured the PTSD had a lot to do with needing to be alone, at sea, man against nature, at least once a day.

Plus, other than the noisy seagulls, it was amazingly quiet out there, and was the perfect place to shut down all the clatter in his life. Whatever it was, surfing was still a lifeline for him, and he needed it. Especially today.

She wiped the counter with a sponge, and he was ready to leave, but something made him stop. It was like his body had quit listening to his brain. *Don't get involved.* "Just call if you need anything, okay?" Now his mouth had gone rogue. Seeing a notepad on the adjacent counter, he scribbled out his cell phone number, then left.

"You might be sorry!" she teasingly called after him.

He already was. Why walk in on someone else's life as a fix-it guy when he had yet to fix his own mess? He really didn't need the frustration.

But when he hit the street, he grinned. Like an idiot. Because he'd just given a woman his phone number for the first time since getting discharged from the service.

* * *

AMERICAN HEROES:
They're coming home—and finding love!

Dear Reader,

I was honored to find out this story had been chosen for the Special Edition American Heroes series in April 2018. When I wrote Mark, I watched and listened to the stories of soldiers who, long after serving their country, were still paying a price, dealing with PTSD. Mark returned home a changed man, and it took the love of his parents, grandfather and brothers, as well as a good woman, to help him finally find peace. He accepted being a different version of himself, stronger for the insight.

The last person in the world Mark expected to fall for was Laurel, the mother of three who moved in across the street. Feeling in over her head starting up the new Prescott B and B while still healing and mourning the loss of her husband, and dealing with her moody teenage son and spirited four-year-old twins, she never expected to fall in love again. Who had time or the inclination?

It's funny how sometimes life steps in and hands people exactly what they need at the worst possible time in their lives. Fortunately, Mark and Laurel were so attracted to each other, they eventually saw through the obstacles and became ready, willing and able to give that unrequested gift of love a real chance.

I hope you'll enjoy this second story in the Delaneys of Sandpiper Beach trilogy. I loved writing it.

Thanks for reading,

Lynne

PS: You can sign up for my newsletter at my website or on my author page at Facebook. Thanks!

Soldier, Handyman, Family Man

Lynne Marshall

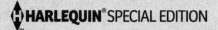
HARLEQUIN® SPECIAL EDITION

Recycling programs
for this product may
not exist in your area.

ISBN-13: 978-1-335-46571-9

Soldier, Handyman, Family Man

Copyright © 2018 by Janet Maarschalk

Printed in U.S.A.

Lynne Marshall used to worry she had a serious problem with daydreaming, and then she discovered she was supposed to write those stories down! A late bloomer, she came to fiction writing after her children were nearly grown. Now she battles the empty nest by writing romantic stories about life, love and happy endings. She's a proud mother and grandmother who loves babies, dogs, books, music and traveling.

Books by Lynne Marshall

Harlequin Special Edition

Her Perfect Proposal
A Doctor for Keeps
The Medic's Homecoming
Courting His Favorite Nurse

The Delaneys of Sandpiper Beach

Forever a Father

Harlequin Medical Romance

Miracle for the Neurosurgeon
A Mother for His Adopted Son
200 Harley Street: American Surgeon in London
Her Baby's Secret Father

Summer Brides

Wedding Date with the Army Doc

The Hollywood Hills Clinic

His Pregnant Sleeping Beauty

Cowboys, Doctors...Daddies!

Hot-Shot Doc, Secret Dad
Father for Her Newborn Baby

Visit the Author Profile page
at Harlequin.com for more titles.

To our true heroes who risk their lives
for their country, their cities, their neighborhoods,
their friends and their families,
and who often pay a personal price.
You have my deepest respect.

Chapter One

The attractive brunette juggling a cardboard box and a plastic trash bag filled with who knew what needed help. Mark Delaney had first noticed her yesterday when her bobbing ponytail had proved to be very distracting. Now, seeing disaster about to happen, he sprang from the ladder, where he painted the underside of The Drumcliffe Hotel roof trim, nearly rolling an ankle. Then he jogged across the street attempting to hide the limp.

"Need help?"

"Oh." She tossed him a flustered glance, the box precariously slipping from her grasp. "Yes, please."

He rushed in and grabbed it, surprised how light it was.

"My favorite English tea set's in there." She used her head to signal the delicate nature of the contents. "Should've thought this through more." She stopped, took a breath and made an obligatory smile. "I'm Laurel Prescott, by the way, and you are?"

"Mark Delaney." With his free hand, he gestured across the street. "My family owns The Drumcliffe."

Her honey-brown brows, a few shades lighter than her hair, lifted. "Ah, so we're neighbors."

He deposited the box on the porch as she came up beside him, then noticed the eyes that were light hazel and shaped like large almonds. He liked that. "Guess so. When are you planning to open the B&B?"

Another inhale, this one deeper. "Good question. My goal is next week, but there are so many last-minute things I need to do, and of course hadn't even thought of." She shook her head rapidly. "Don't know what I was thinking doing this final move the week school started." She hoisted the trash bag over her shoulder. Something clanked inside. "Oh, yes, I do—I'd finally have a few hours to myself!"

He couldn't help but laugh with her even if it was over impending hysteria. "Anything else you need carried in?"

Her downright attractive eyes sparkled, signaling he may as well have been sent from heaven. Which felt good for a change.

"Are you sure you have the time? I mean it's obvious you're in the middle of painting."

He glanced down at his black T-shirt and jeans, both splattered with the eggshell paint his mother had meticulously picked for the trim. "I was ready for a break anyway." Then he looked across the road where he'd left the lid off the paint can. "Just give me a second, okay?"

"Of course!" She continued up the steps to the grand Queen Anne–styled Victorian house, which had been sitting empty, according to his mother, for ages. Some nice old couple used to live there when he was a kid, right up to the time he'd left home. He remembered once having the best apple pie he'd ever eaten in that kitchen.

He crossed the street heading back to the hotel. For the last several months, he'd seen crews inside and out bringing the gem back to its original beauty and then some. By the extensive upgrades, he knew his mother had been right about the old home being turned into a bed-and-breakfast. The workers had finished a few weeks back, making the steeply pitched roof with the dominant front gable and oddly shaped porch look picture-book perfect. Once a blah blue with ho-hum white trim, chipped and peeling from years of neglect, now the house was sage green with cream trim and forest green detailing between the cornices, and Mark had to admit it looked classy. Like her. That had been his first impression of his new neighbor last week when she'd stopped by to check on the finishing touches.

The lady was way out of his league, so today, when she was dressed in work clothes—faded straight-legged jeans with slip-in rubber-soled shoes, and a stretched-out polo shirt that'd seen better days—it made him smile. She fit right in with his style. And for the second day in a row she'd worn a ponytail. Not that he was keeping tabs or anything, but man, the ponytail was distracting.

Mark replaced the lid on the paint can.

"Little early for a break isn't it?" Padraig Delaney chided his middle grandson, while he had no doubt just finished a Monday morning round at the city course judging by his loud patterned golf slacks and a salmon-colored shirt. His daily routine at eighty-five kept his craggy face tanned and his blue eyes bright, not to mention the notorious toothy grin pasted in place. Which he was currently flashing since noticing where Mark had come from and the lady across the street waiting for him.

Mark smiled at his grandda with the Guinness-soaked voice and tendency toward magical thinking. They had an understanding since both had known how it felt to be young, far away from home, frightened and lonely—though one in peacetime and the other, well, in that hot mess known as the Middle East. Yet that was their unspoken bond, and nothing would break it.

Everyone knew Padraig Delaney's history. As a young Irish immigrant in the 1950s, he'd been brought over to work the new and lush golf courses along the central California coast. Cheap labor for sure, but he'd also had the foresight to scrimp and save money and buy the small patch of land in Sandpiper Beach. As his jobs and responsibility advanced, he saved more and worked like the devil to build the humble hotel back in the late sixties and early seventies. If it weren't for that hardworking dreamer's spirit, who knew what the Delaney clan would be up to now? So he'd cut him some slack over playing golf every morning. The man had earned it.

As Mark always did, he also tolerated the supernosy man's inclinations. "I'll get 'er done. All of it. By the end of the day. Have a good game?"

"Every game's a good game, Marky my boy, 'cuz I'm alive."

Mark had heard a similar statement from his grandfather at some point every single day since he'd returned from Afghanistan last year. He understood it was a less-than-subtle message, but most of the time he couldn't relate to it. Though today, glancing across the street to the lady with the ponytail, his personal outlook struck him as somewhat optimistic. "That it is, Grandda. That it is." He stood, ready to set off again for the B&B and the woman who needed some serious help.

"Fraternizing with the competition are ye?" Ah, he wasn't going to let this slip by.

Mark laughed, knowing Grandda was making a joke. His mother was the one and *only* person in the family fretting about the B&B opening. Padraig Delaney understood different types stayed at a place like that than their modestly priced hotel. The B&B wasn't about competition, it was about revitalizing the town, which would be good for everyone. "Just helping out a neighbor."

"A mighty attractive neighbor I might add." The old man winked.

Mark returned a let's-not-go-there stare, though Grandda already had.

"Have you thought more about taking over the hotel?" So he'd gotten Mark's hint and changed the subject.

"You know I'm not ready to do that." He placed the paint can next to the hotel wall, then folded the ladder and put that next to it. "Besides, Mom and Dad really don't want to retire yet." At least he hoped so.

"Could fool me, the way they talk about it mornin' till night. Besides, you're the only one who loves this hotel the same way I do."

Mark couldn't deny that he was the logical person to pick up where his parents left off, if they retired like they kept threatening to. With Daniel being a doctor with his own practice and Conor a deputy sheriff for the county with plans for advancement, neither brother showed the slightest interest in running the place. But since being honorably discharged from the army last year, he'd wanted nothing to do with responsibility. For now, being a handyman every morning and surfing every afternoon was about all he thought he could handle. Still he did have a vision for The Drumcliffe, which he'd talked to his parents about under the condition that they would give him time, and postpone any immediate plans to retire. If Grandda caught on, he might insist Mark take on more responsibility right away. But he flat out wasn't ready. Yet.

Mark kept his head down, rather than pursue the pointed conversation about the future of the family hotel. Grandda cleared his throat in resignation, but Mark knew there would be future dialogue on the subject. The man would probably hound him until he gave in. It might even be for his own good.

"Well, I'm off, then." Padraig set out heading up Main Street for his daily visit with the other local business owners, using an ancient wood putter as a cane. "Remember the selkie, lad," he said, not bothering to look back for Mark's reaction, knowing it would be annoyed.

Would the old man ever let go of the notion Mark and his brothers had saved a selkie the day they'd gone deep-sea fishing together? First off, it wasn't a selkie, it was a *seal* that was being hunted by a pod of orca. Foolish or not, the brothers had used the fishing boat to interfere with the obvious training session for a young orca on how to catch a snack. Turns out they'd distracted the pod just long enough for the seal to escape. Their biggest mistake, after risking getting their boat flipped by ticked-off orcas, was repeating the story during the Sunday night family dinner in the pub. You'd have thought they'd saved the king of the little people judging by their grandfather's reaction. *The seal was a selkie,* he'd said.

The selkie now owes each of you a favor. As if he knew the selkie rulebook backward and forward.

Ever since, Padraig Delaney, a wise and intelligent man on many other levels, but obviously not this one, insisted each brother would find true love.

Right. And there's always a pot of gold at the end of a rainbow. Anyone ever find it?

His oldest brother, Daniel, hadn't helped Grandda's notion a bit when he'd hired Keela and, after a few months, started dating her. Now they were newly married with a baby on the way, and calling that proof, Grandda had doubled down on his woo-woo predictions. Especially after he'd had a Guinness or two. He'd gaze over his glass and give Mark, the middle brother, and Conor, the baby, meaningful glances meant to convey they'd be next. What a load of malarkey.

"Remember the selkie, my ass," Mark mumbled, watching the old man stride up the street without a care. What had made him bring *that* up again, anyway?

Because their new neighbor was a knockout, that's why. Mark smiled to himself. So Grandda had noticed, too.

And with that undeniable thought, he grinned and cleaned his hands with the rag hanging on the ladder and headed back across the way, even though she wasn't likely to give him the time of day after he'd finished helping her. He was still just a fix-it guy.

Laurel walked back to her car and secretly watched Mark reseal a paint can when an old gentleman approached him.

Here she was, thirty-five, a widow second-guessing her every move. Being the mother of a teenage boy dealing with grief and anger on top of the usual teen angst, and twin four-year-olds just beginning their journey with school, only added to the doubt. Buying the old house with one of Alan's generous insurance policies had been a risk, for sure, but it had also been her way of beginning again. Lord knew she needed a fresh start. They all did. The last five years had been hijacked by Alan's cancer, then remissions, praying the worst had been over, followed by the nightmare two years later of those demon cells' return. If anyone deserved a do-over it was the Prescott family. Though Alan never got the luxury of a second chance.

She swallowed a hard and familiar lump. Life had been difficult without him the past two years, and may have kicked the wind out of her, but now she wanted to move on. What choice did she have, really?

She retrieved a few small items from the trunk of the car and subtly watched on the periphery, the conversation going on across the street at the hotel between the old golfer and Mark, her disturbingly attractive neighbor. The fact she'd noticed him was progress, wasn't it? He was good-looking. There, she'd admitted it. But so what?

Before the move, she'd been walking around in a trance, dealing with the lowest rung on the Maslow hierarchy of needs—excluding sex, of course. That rarely entered her mind, except on those nights when she missed Alan's touch so badly she cried. All she wanted to do was build a new life for her family, to keep them safe and fed, healthy, while wondering if this B&B had been the best idea she'd ever had or the craziest.

Regardless, she owned the Queen Anne–styled house in Sandpiper Beach and planned to become a small businesswoman. A full-time job outside the home would provide a paycheck, but it would also keep her

away from the ones she wanted to look after. This so-
lution, buying and running a B&B, was the next best
way she knew how to provide for her kids.

She glanced across the street. Why was that man so
distracting? She had a world of other things to think
about, didn't need a single distraction, yet there he was,
tall, dark hair, intense blue eyes, totally Irish American. Younger than her.

She walked back to the house, trying not to look
over her shoulder. What could be the harm in allowing
a tiny, secret attraction for someone who lived across
the street? Could she go so far as labeling it a crush, or
merely an interest? Whichever, she'd felt something the
very first time she'd spotted him. Why now? Could it
be a signal that, after two years of living in limbo, she
was finally ready to move on with life?

Maybe.

A half hour later, after passing each other with arms
loaded on trips back and forth to the house, with nothing
more than glances and respectful smiles, Mark carried
the last of Laurel's boxes up the porch steps.

The grand entrance and main sitting room were de-
tailed and updated with fresh paint, crown molding, a
traditional fireplace, ornate mantel and rich wood bal-
ustrades lining the otherwise modest staircase. But the
impressive dining room with its long and grand oak
table, antique print wallpaper and classic crystal chandelier was clearly the focal point. Visitors were going
to love this old house.

"Looks great," was all he said.

"Thank you," she said with an earnest gaze. "I'm
petrified. After all the money I've sunk into it, what if
it's a big bomb?"

"Have you done this before?" He also wondered if she was married, which bothered him. Why should he care?

"Never." Something close to panic flashed in her eyes, but she recovered quickly. "Can I get you some lemonade? It's the least I can do for all your help." *Maybe she's divorced.*

He wasn't the type to stick around and chat. In fact, he'd kept mostly to himself in the year since he'd been back from Afghanistan, skipping socializing outside of his family, but something nudged him to accept her offer. "Sounds good. Thanks."

He followed her into the modest-sized kitchen for a house this big, and took in the view from the updated double-paned back window. The beach and ocean weren't far off, and he assumed most of the guest rooms would have views of the same. "I wouldn't worry too much about bombing out. Unless you overprice the rooms."

"I've done my homework on pricing," she said, opening the double-wide stainless steel refrigerator and grabbing a pitcher of lemonade. He also noticed she'd gone the modern route with the appliances and the long marble-covered island. Seemed like an efficiency decision, if she planned the usual serving of breakfast for her guests. "I'm right in the middle of the current going rate. Except for the honeymoon suite, of course." She gave a flirty wistful glance. "It's beautiful and well worth the price."

He didn't get what the deal was with rooms that were supposed to enhance romance—seemed to him you either had it or you didn't—but figured Laurel was depending on other people who did. Whereas The Drumcliffe appealed more to families and seniors on budgets. So he was content to leave the "lover's weekend packages" for her B&B. More power to her. Though Mom adamantly voiced the need for their hotel to have broader appeal, and she'd been on a quest to start wedding packages maximizing the gorgeous view and their large lawn area right along the ocean. An idea popped into his head: Why not turn the biggest room with the best view at the hotel into a honeymoon suite? Maybe he could get some ideas for decorating from Laurel. Of course, that would only mean more on his ever-growing to-do list. Which reminded him he was supposed to start building an arbor today, and a gazebo after that.

She handed him a dainty hand-painted glass of lemonade. So instead of gulping like he'd intended from thirst, he took only a sip of the fresh lemon and hint-of-mint liquid. "This tastes great."

"Thanks. I made it myself using the Meyer lemons from the side yard."

"Really good." The yard, he'd noticed, needed some serious trimming and weeding. But she'd probably already made plans with a gardener for that, so he didn't offer his services. Why would he? Besides, he had enough going on with the hotel.

He sensed she had all kinds of extra-special tricks up her sleeve where the B&B was concerned, like this homemade lemonade, and figured her guests would return because of those extra-special touches. That was if they found the house in the first place. "You have plans for a grand opening or something?"

She took a drink, her lashes fluttering. "I plan to run some ads and have an open house."

"That's a good idea."

She looked gratefully at him. "I grew up in Pismo Beach, so I know we have a long season. Does it ever get really dead around here?"

"I've only been back the past year, so I'm not a great resource. I'll check with my parents, if you'd like."

"Oh, sorry, I just assumed you—"

"—I was in the service for ten years. My parents run the hotel. I'm still getting used to being back." Would that matter to her, that he wasn't the guy in charge? Again, he chided, why should he care?

He'd left home at twenty-one an accomplished surfer, surf bum as Grandda often teased. Then he'd come back after a few tours in the Middle East, mostly Afghanistan, but also in Iraq, someone he didn't recognize anymore. He'd dealt with his mood swings in his own way, spending the last year withdrawn, just trying to get his bearings in the real world again, while working on the hotel. And surfing. It had all been part of his healing journey, as the VA therapist had suggested. That was the reason he and his brothers had been fishing the day of the "selkie" incident. A bonding trip, they'd called it. But in truth, Daniel and Conor were worried about him and had wanted to help him over the slump he'd slipped into. Some trip that'd turned out to be. He still wasn't 100 percent past PTSD. Still had occasional nightmares, hated being in big crowds, but he was on the road back to being a combination of the guy he used to be and the man he'd become. Less outgoing, more inclined to think things through before acting. Less lighthearted, grimmer. Someone he'd have to get used to. Maybe all thirty-one-year-olds went through the same thing?

Laurel studied him, those caramel eyes subtly moving around his face, her mind probably wondering what his story was. Well, she wasn't the only one with questions. "What brought you here?"

"Oh." Obviously unprepared for him to turn the tables. "I missed the beach. After college I got married and moved inland to Paso Robles to raise my family. Then I lost my husband a couple years ago."

"I'm sorry." And he meant it, even though he could only imagine how horrible it would be to lose someone you loved.

She quietly inhaled, then took another sip of lemonade. "Yeah. It's been rough."

That was something he could relate to, the rough part. He wasn't good at this sort of thing, sympathy or empathy or whatever it was called, but he honestly felt bad for her. She had a lot going on, and a big project like opening a B&B all alone was probably as stressful as it got for a person. There went that nudging sensation again. "If you need any help, I'm around." *What happened to being too busy?*

"Thank you." She looked sincere and grateful. "I'll definitely take you up on that offer."

Good. A decisive and wise woman. But, out of character, he'd just opened a door he wasn't sure that (a) he had time for or (b) he wanted to go through. Yet. She might be single, but she had a family, for crying out loud.

Her appreciative eyes suddenly widened. She frantically looked at her wrist. "Oh, no! It's time to pick up the girls." She grabbed her purse and rushed for the door. "It's their first day at school. Kindergarten! I can't be late."

He followed, then noticed she had to work extra hard to get the front door locked. "I'll come back later and have a look at that lock, if you want."

She flashed another earnest gaze, this one accompanied with a pretty smile, which caught him off guard. "That'd be great!"

Then off she ran for her white minivan, where identical car seats were installed in the back—such a total mom.

Man, he must be completely out of his antisocial mind, because somehow, he found the whole entrepreneur—and multitasking-mother bit—sexy as hell. And that was way off course for his current game plan—keeping a low profile and figuring out where he fit in life...or even if he wanted to.

Laurel kept to the speed limit, but barely, trying desperately to get the image of Mark Delaney out of her head. Did he have any idea how gorgeous he was? Dark brown hair combed straight back from his forehead and just long enough to curl under his ears, clear blue eyes, a two-day growth of beard with the hint of red in the sideburn whiskers. His black T-shirt stretched across a broad chest and shoulders, with a peekaboo tear along his sleek abs, and arms that qualified for a construction worker calendar. His faded black jeans had matching tears at the knees from hard work, not superficial fashion, and fit his slim hips and long legs like he'd been born in them. Damn he was hot! Whether he realized it or not was the question. He certainly didn't act "all that." In fact, there was something dark and tender about him that put her at ease. And that ease put her on edge.

Laurel glanced at her face in the rearview mirror, horror soon overtaking her. She'd been looking like that? Her hair in a messy ponytail, not a stitch of makeup. Not even lip gloss. The man probably thought of her as a poor, struggling aunt.

She slammed on the brakes, nearly missing a red light. *Woman, get a hold of yourself! You're thirty-five, obviously older than him, and not to mention the mother of three. It doesn't matter how you look, he's not interested.* Still, there was much to appreciate about Mark Delaney, and she wasn't blind—or dead—in that department. Yet. Sometimes she thought she might be, so he was a pleasant surprise, after all she'd been through. She tugged the elastic out of her hair and let it fall to her shoulders.

Pulling into the parking lot, she prayed she hadn't cut it too close and that her kids wouldn't be the last ones there. They'd dealt with enough abandonment issues losing their father two years ago, and having to live as if the hospital was their second home for a year before that. Now was their time to get back to living a regular life, and nothing would get in Laurel's way of giving that to her kids. A quick thought of her fourteen-year-old son, Peter, made her chest pinch, but now wasn't the time to go there. She had to pick up her girls.

She parked and jogged into the kindergarten classroom. Gracie and Claire were happily playing puzzles with the little girl they'd met on Welcome to Kindergarten night, who wore a cast. *Anna was it?*

"Can Anna come home with us? Her mom's late, too." Claire, the oldest by twelve minutes, and clearly the bossiest, spoke first.

"I don't think the school lets kids go home with just anyone." Laurel used her diplomatic-mother voice.

"Stranger danger!" Gracie piped up.

"We're not strangers," Claire corrected, as she always did with Gracie. "Remember, we played together before." She used her middle finger to slide her pink glasses up her tiny nose.

"I pre-member. Do you, Annie?"

"It's Anna." Claire the clarifier simply couldn't help herself. "And *re*-member."

During Alan's long remission from the first bout of leukemia, and nearly a decade since Peter had been born, no one had been more shocked to discover she was pregnant with twins than Laurel. But life had always been crazy that way.

When Alan relapsed with a vengeance when the girls were a year old, everyone had been so distracted that Gracie's chronic ear problems had gotten way out of hand before Laurel had taken her to the pediatrician. She'd been walking around with fluid in her inner ears, which had affected her hearing. It was like listening to people speak underwater and had slowed her speech, while Claire seemed to have been born chatting, and now speaking for and chronically correcting her twin. Since having tubes inserted, Gracie's hearing had improved, but she still often got words wrong. Claire never let her forget it, either.

"Oh, there you are, Anna." A breathless voice with a distinct accent spoke from behind. "Sorry I'm late, sweetness."

"That's okay, Mom, these are my friends."

The woman introduced herself to Laurel as Keela. "Thank you for staying with Anna. I don't want to be accused of running on Irish time, but we had a walk-in at the clinic and it threw things sideways."

Delighted by Keela's Irish accent, Laurel grinned. In the week she'd been in town, she'd already heard about the Delaney Physical Medicine Clinic from one of the women at the local farmers' market, who'd told her, after chatting and discovering Laurel's B&B was right across Main Street from The Drumcliffe, about Daniel's recent marriage to an "Irish girl." Small town. News traveled fast.

"I just got here myself. Honestly, I don't think the girls missed us a bit."

"Probably right."

"We should set up a playdate some afternoon," Laurel suggested, keeping in mind Keela worked full-time.

"T'would be *grand*. Maybe a Saturday would be best."

Ms. Juanita, the young teacher not much taller than her students, wandered over. "Are we all ready now?" she asked diplomatically, dropping the major hint it was past time to leave. So they did. But not before exchanging phone numbers.

As promised, later that afternoon after he'd finished painting the trim and had gotten a good start on the arbor, Mark headed back over to Laurel's B&B with his toolbox in hand. He planned to fix her lock. One of the benefits of being raised around a hotel was learning to be a jack-of-all-trades. *Otherwise we'd go bankrupt,* as his father used to say when he and his brothers griped about spending their Saturday afternoons working around the hotel. It'd always been extra torture when the surf was up and he'd been itching to hit those waves.

Laurel was in the front yard, and two young girls in matching striped leggings and navy blue tops sat on the porch steps, though one wore glasses. Looking stressed, Laurel faced off with a scrawny kid by the yard gate who was somewhere in the early teen stage and who hadn't yet grown into his nose. He wore cargo shorts and an oversize, ancient-looking T-shirt with a picture of Bart Simpson on the front. Shaggy dark brown waves in an obvious growing-out stage consumed his ears and partially covered his eyes. He leaned forward, confronting her, his mouth tight and chin jutted out.

Mark thought about turning around, leaving them to their personal business, but their heated interchange, and the fact her hair was down and blowing with the breeze, prodded him to keep going. Maybe she could use some backup.

"Peter, I've got too much on my plate right now."

"I'm sick of having to drag those pests around." His voice warbled between boy and man, cracking over *those pests*.

"We're not pests!" The little one with glasses sounded indignant.

"Not pets!" the thinner of the two incorrectly echoed, garnering a confused glance from her twin.

"I need you to watch the girls while I do some errands. Is that too much to ask?"

"I'm sick of being their babysitter."

The fair-haired girls looked like twins. Identical twins, but with the help of one wearing glasses and one being slightly smaller, to tell them apart. The glasses girl took it upon herself to move in on the ongoing argument. "Sing with us, Peter. Please?" A future peace activist, no doubt.

"Pleee-sio?" Little Miss Echo being creative?

Without waiting, they started singing "Where Is Thumbkin" using their fingers and acting out the verses, oblivious, while Laurel and Peter continued to square off.

"You know it'll take me twice as long if I bring them."

"Don't care."

What should he do now? Just walk right up and pretend he didn't have a clue they were fighting? He slowed down. That seemed lame.

"Okay, I'm not asking, I'm *telling* you to stay here."

"I need time by myself!" Peter pounded his fist on his chest while his voice cracked again. "You're the one who told me to get out and explore the neighborhood! Meet kids my age."

Ten feet away from the picket fence and gate, Mark stopped. If anyone could understand the need to be by himself, Mark could. Hell, he'd been the king of withdrawal when he'd first come home. The girls continued singing and gesturing—*"Where is pointer, where is pointer...?"*

"I need your help." Laurel wouldn't back down.

"I'm leaving!"

Mark figured it must be damn hard to lose a father when a boy needed him most, but it still bothered him the kid was taking his anger out on his mother. He decided to step in, offer Laurel some support. "Is this a bad time?"

"Oh, Mark." Laurel looked flustered and frustrated, her cheeks flushed. Those soft hazel-brown eyes from earlier now dark and tense. Edging toward the street side of the gate, Peter stepped backward, gearing up for his escape.

"How are you today, sir?" the twins sang louder.

Mark stepped closer, giving Peter a forced but friendly smile, hoping to keep him from taking off. "I'm Mark. Nice to meet you."

In response, he received a death glare. It was clear the kid was furious, not just about Mark butting in, or his mother demanding he pull his share of responsibility, but about life in general. About how sucky it must be when a dad dies.

Unaware, the girls kept singing their nursery rhyme. *"Run away. Run away."* Their way of coping with stress?

Still glowering, Peter spoke verse three. *"Where is tall man?"* He added the middle-finger gesture for the sake of his mother and Mark, made sure they both saw it clearly, then took off running, flip-flops flapping, down the street toward the beach.

"Peter!" Laurel yelled, anger flashing in those eyes.

He thought about running after Peter and straightening him out, but stopped the urge. It wasn't his place.

It took guts, or total desperation, to flip off a complete stranger in front of his mother, he'd give Peter that. He didn't envy Laurel's having to deal with that on top of opening the B&B. Guests didn't go to places like this to hear family arguments. Yet Laurel was a widow with three kids to take care of, and the proprietor of an about-to-open business. After he fixed her lock, he'd steer clear.

Laurel called after Peter again. When Peter didn't stop or turn around, she dug fingers into her hair, obviously torn about whether to run after him or let him go. The girls had stopped singing, now zeroing in on their mother and gathering close to her. She put a hand on both of them, giving a motherly rub and pat, which immediately eased the tension in their sparrow-sized shoulders. Then she steered them back toward the porch.

Looking downcast, but not defeated, Laurel glanced back at Mark. "Welcome to my world."

Chapter Two

Ten minutes later, Mark kept to himself as he tested the key that Laurel had given him in the stubborn front door lock. The scene with Peter had been unpleasant to say the least, and he'd had to bite his tongue to keep from butting in and telling the kid what he thought. Really thought—*listen, punk, you don't talk to your mother like that. Ever!* But it wasn't his place, and keeping it real, he'd heard a similar warning—without the punk part—from his father a long time ago. Disrespecting parents must be some teen rite of passage. From the way Laurel had mostly kept her cool, she'd probably been down that road with Peter before.

While he fiddled with the lock, Laurel went about distracting the little ones with a snack and a promise to watch one afternoon kid's show. He was pretty sure "yay" meant they'd accepted her deal.

A minute later, he'd squirted powdered graphite into

the keyhole, moved the key in and out a few times, then retested the sticky mechanism. The lock opened and closed just fine. For good measure, he repeated the process on the bolt lock, since her guests would most likely be using their keys after hours, and Laurel might appreciate their not waking her up to get in.

Before The Drumcliffe had switched to card keys, he and his brothers had become experts with fixing sticky locks. They'd learned the hard way that vegetable oil and WD-40 helped for the short term, but eventually made the problem worse. Then they'd discovered graphite, the non-gummy way to fix a lock.

On his knees with the door open, Mark surreptitiously watched Laurel wander his way, carrying a small plate of cookies. She sat on the nearest rocker in the row along the porch, stretching out her sleek legs, then offering him the plate.

"Do you barter?" she toyed, waiting for him to catch on.

"Work for chocolate chip cookies? You bet." He took one and popped it whole into his mouth. *Holy melting deliciousness*, it was good. "Pretty sure I got the better deal, too." He should've waited until he'd finished chewing and swallowing. He probably still had chocolate teeth.

She laughed gently. At least he'd done that for her. Made her smile. And a nice one it was, too, wide, straight and lighting up her eyes.

"You know he's grieving, right?" she said, growing serious, her eyes seeking his, needing him to understand why her kid had shot off his mouth earlier.

"I figured something was going on. I get the impression a lady like you wouldn't put up with that behavior otherwise."

She put her head against the back of the rocker, nibbling on a cookie. "He blames me for everything. Sometimes I think he even blames me for his father getting cancer."

"From what I recall, being a teenager is hard enough. Losing a parent on top of it, well, that's got to bite. Hard."

"He was only twelve when Alan died, but for so many years before that, Alan's being ill was the focal point of our family. He missed out on a lot of things other kids his age took for granted. And the insecurity of it all, that I know firsthand. Must have been devastating for him, because it nearly killed me."

Moved by her opening up so easily, Mark sat on his heels, wanting to give back, to make this an interchange somehow, but he was out of practice. "He's, what, fourteen now?"

She gave a thoughtful nod without looking at him, taking another small bite of cookie. "Who invented adolescent angst, anyway?"

Mark made one quick laugh. "He probably doesn't know how to move on. Maybe he's in a rut and needs a nudge or something." This conversation had edged into familiar personal territory. He could say the same thing about himself—not sure how to move on, feeling in a rut—but for the sake of Laurel he focused on her problem and her son.

"We've tried therapy. He went to a teen grief group for a while. Then he stopped. I couldn't bring myself to force him to go." She glanced at Mark for understanding. He assented. "I think he's afraid of his feelings. He's hurt so much for so long, he can't imagine going over everything again, examining the pain of losing his dad." She sighed. "I don't know." Now she looked at him, really looked at him, her eyes searching his, waking up some dark and forgotten place. Did she sense his pain? "And you probably never thought you'd get sucked into my family problems when you offered to help fix my locks today, did you?"

He pushed out a smile, just for her, because he figured she could use a friendly face right about now. Sticking to the superficial, rather than let himself *feel* something, he concentrated on how her hair looked resting on her shoulders. "It's okay. Every family has issues."

She lifted her brows, in a prove-it kind of way, but soon exchanged that for a quizzical expression. "I have no idea why I'm telling you my life story." She leveled him with a stare. "Just strike that part, okay?"

"No worries. You feel like talking, go right ahead." A long moment followed where they quietly assessed each other, and she must have decided she'd spilled her guts enough for the day. She took another bite of her cookie, which, for some crazy reason, looked sexier than it should. He couldn't take the intimacy of watching her mouth, or sharing concerns and feelings, especially if she expected him to open up about himself or his family in return. So he deliberately changed the topic. "And if you give me another cookie, I'll throw in checking all the guest room locks."

As though relieved, she smiled, pushing the plate toward him. "It's a deal."

As he went through the rest of the house, he noticed all six of the guest rooms were on the second floor. Laurel and the kids must have taken up residence on the first floor, in the back part of the house.

Out of the blue he wondered what she'd look like with that top layer of stress erased from her pretty face. And then he stopped himself from going a single thought further. What was the point? She had her hands full, and the last thing he needed was to pursue a woman with kids.

He grabbed his small workbag, went downstairs and found Laurel in the kitchen slicing apples and carrots. He stopped for a second to enjoy the view.

"I'm all done here." He set the small bottle of graphite on the long central island. "If you have any more problems with locks, just use this."

She stopped slicing. "Thanks so much."

In rushed the twins. "We're hungry," Claire, the spokesperson, said.

"Yeah, my tummy's qweezin'," said Gracie.

She tossed them both a piece of carrot and apple. Surprisingly, they accepted her offer and scuttled off for the backyard like contented bunnies. Intuition must be part of the job description for a mom. Another thing about her that impressed him.

"You may be wondering about Gracie's speech."

"She does have an interesting way of saying things."

Laurel sighed as she leaned forward, elbows and forearms resting on the kitchen island countertop. The pose shouldn't be appealing, but it was. "During Alan's illness, I was so caught up in his needs, I didn't realize that Gracie's unusual speech was a sign she had fluid in her ears. I thought it was baby talk. It wasn't until after Alan died I snapped out of my trance and took them both to the pediatrician. Gracie needed tubes in her ears, and Claire flunked her three-year-old vision test. I didn't have a clue about either of them."

She looked defeated, and it bothered him. "You had a lot on your plate. The main thing, nothing was life-threatening and you fixed the problem." *Listen to me,*

Mr. Logical. He stepped closer to her end of the island. "Maybe quit being so hard on yourself?"

She blinked and sighed. "I might have to hire you as a life coach."

"Ha! First you'd have to find *me* one."

"And what's your story?" Her inquisitive stare nearly pushed him off balance.

"Ten years in the army. Tours in Iraq and Afghanistan. Need I say more?"

She looked horrified at first. That was the only way Mark could explain her expression, then it changed.

They gazed at each other, her manner seeming sympathetic, understanding. Mark was almost positive she thought the same thing—they were two people who'd come through tough times humbled and haggard. He'd worked out a drill to deal with his, but had she?

Mark's usual routine was to work all morning and through the early afternoon, then grab his board and head down to the beach to catch a few waves. What used to be his passion had now become his solace, better than a doctor's prescription or a cold beer. Funny how time changed things like that—passion to solace. He figured the PTSD had a lot to do with needing to be alone, at sea, man against nature, at least once a day. Plus, other than the noisy seagulls, it was amazingly quiet out there, and was the perfect place to shut down all the clatter in his life. Whatever it was, surfing was still a lifeline for him and he needed it. Especially today.

She wiped the counter with a sponge, and he was ready to leave, but something made him stop. It was like his body had quit listening to his brain. Don't get involved. "Just call if you need anything, okay?" Now his mouth had gone rogue. Seeing a notepad on the adjacent counter, he scribbled out his cell phone number, then left.

"You might be sorry!" she teasingly called after him.

He already was. Why walk in on someone else's life as a fix-it guy, when he'd yet to fix his own mess? He really didn't need the frustration.

But when he hit the street, he grinned. Like an idiot. Because he'd just given a woman his phone number for the first time since getting discharged from the service.

A half hour later, dressed in red board shorts and an old stretched-out, holey T-shirt, with surfboard under his arm, Mark strode toward the beach where the sun cast a golden orange tint on the ocean. Being the middle Delaney brother, he'd opted out of the role of peacekeeper by default early on. Instead, he'd elected to become an attention-getting surfer. It'd paid off in spades, too. Popularity. Girlfriends. Respect.

He'd intended to sign up for the army right after high school, but his father and mother had convinced him to try the local community college first. He did, without an inkling of what he wanted to major in, for two years, but didn't get a degree because the classes he took didn't add up to one major's requirements. Then that faraway Middle East war got personal. A good friend since grammar school had been killed in Iraq. It might not have been logical thinking, but after that he felt called to serve, so, without his parents' blessings, he'd enlisted. After voting in a presidential election for the first time, signing up for the army had been his next major life decision. And he was still re-adjusting to civilian life.

A predictable afternoon breeze had kicked up and the water was choppy, but he smiled at the swelling of sets forming in the distance. A few of the usual guys in wet suits were out there, most of them half his age. They'd probably been there all day. One with long sun-bleached hair caught the next wave, road the crest, then wiped out.

Halfway down the beach, he passed a group of loud teenagers talking trash to someone. He turned his head to check things out. Five guys ranging from tall and buff to short and heavy, wearing board shorts and brand-name skateboarder T-shirts, were getting their jollies by bullying someone much smaller. He looked closer, saw the shaggy brown hair, the nose he was still grow-ing into and that oversize T-shirt with Bart Simpson on the front. It was Peter with a frown cast in iron on his face, staring at his flip-flops. Obviously hating every second, he let the jerks taunt and tease him, but what choice did he have, one against five?

Mark dropped his board and headed their way. "Hey, Peter, I was lookin' for you, man! It's time for your surfing lesson."

Peter looked up, surprised. So did the other kids.

He walked right up to the group as if everything was A-OK, but making eye contact with the leader let him know he understood what was going on and it was ending right now.

One perk—or pain, depending on what kind of mood he was in—of being Sandpiper's very own surfing champion was the whole town knew him. His first-place regional championship trophy and a larger-than-life pic-ture of him at eighteen with awful peroxided hair, at the height of his competition days, were on display at the local high school. He'd been the captain of the Sand-piper High surf team—hell, he'd been the guy to orga-nize the team—and had led them to regional victories for two years. Then he'd moved on to statewide and a few national competitions where more was at risk, but with respectable success. From the reaction of these losers and tough-guy wannabes, even they knew who he was. Or used to be.

"We wus just horsin' around with the new kid."

"Didn't know he knew you." The tallest nudged Peter toward Mark.

"Yeah, I'm mentoring Peter. He's a natural. See you *boys* around," he said, making sure the kids understood he'd be watching them, and escorted Peter toward his board. So much for not getting involved.

"Want to tell me what was going on?" he asked when they'd retrieved the board and, out of earshot, were heading toward the ocean.

"I was just sitting on the beach, reading a book on my phone and they came out of nowhere. Started giving me a hard time. Bully a-holes."

"Punks are always gonna be punks."

"Nah. They think I'm a nerd because I'm different. I'm skinny and I've got a big nose." His anger radiated toward Mark, making the ocean air seem thicker. They walked on.

Mark also understood, since talking to Laurel, that Peter was still grieving and working through the stress of losing his father, which also made him an easy mark. For some reason, jerks had special radar for vulnerable kids. "Hey, first off, they should talk, if that's the reason. Did you look at them? Listen, it could be something as dumb as the fact you're the new kid and they know you don't have any friends yet to stick up for you, which will change soon enough."

"And I keep getting stuck watching my sisters. It's not exactly cool to hang out with four-year-olds."

So that was why he'd put up such a fight earlier with Laurel. Mark figured it was worth mentioning to her. In the meantime, he'd practice treating the boy like a young friend.

"Yeah, but I bet girls love that, in an 'aw' kind of way."

Peter screwed up his face, like Mark had said the dumbest thing in the world.

"What's with the Bart shirt, man? He back in style?"

"It was my dad's." Peter looked at his chest as if reconsidering the meaning.

What was he supposed to say to that? The kid still missed his father. They continued on, quiet for another few moments, watching the waves as they strolled.

"Well, now that I've announced you're my student, I guess we better get started. Take Bart off. You got trunks under those cargos?"

Peter nodded.

"Wearin' sunscreen?"

He nodded again, but Mark suspected it was a fib, so he grabbed the small bottle from his back pocket. They both put it on.

"Let's hit the waves."

Whether it was because Peter was shaken up from what had just transpired and was grateful, or the kid had always secretly wanted to learn to surf, Mark hadn't a clue, but highly out of character, from what Mark had witnessed of Peter so far, he did what he was told. And gladly!

After the initial "how to" lesson, and a discussion of strength and balance exercises Peter needed to do to get into shape for surfing, Mark used the time waiting for waves, both sitting on the board, to get to know a little about Peter. "Where'd you go to school last year?"

"Paso Robles Middle School."

"What's your favorite subject?"

"Art, I guess."

"Are you good at it?"

"Kind of."

"Have a girlfriend?"

He got a killer "as if" glare for that.

"Who's your best friend?"

Peter stared down at the board, silent.

"No friend?"

"My dad was sick all the time, okay?"

Mark didn't react to the kid spitting the words at him. He could only imagine how hard it would be to maintain a friendship when his world was wrapped tight with worry and a fatally sick father. Or maybe parents were hesitant to let their sons sleep over at Peter's house, like cancer was contagious or something. Who knew. "Must've been hard."

"I hated it. I mean I loved him, but everything was so crappy all the time."

Now they were getting somewhere. Peter's guard was coming down. "I hear ya. Must have been a bitch."

"They made me go to some stupid group. We were all a bunch of losers."

"You mean you'd all lost someone you loved?" He needed to reframe it for Peter—something Mark himself had learned when he went into group therapy—because he couldn't let Peter get away with the negative opinion of himself and other grievers, or anyone in therapy.

The kid's mouth was tight, in a straight line, and he looked on the verge of crying.

"This anger you're feeling all the time is real. It's part of grieving. When we lose someone we love, we grieve for them. Sometimes it makes us angry as hell."

"How do you know?" He spit out the words, challenging Mark.

"I lost more military buddies than I care to count in Iraq and Afghanistan. I know what I'm talking about." His grief had been the single hardest part of coming back to Sandpiper Beach, because he no longer had the distraction of fighting a war. He was faced head-on with all the loss and horrifying memories. They'd crashed against him every single day and knocked him down. Made him want to either strike out or withdraw, so he chose to pull back, lie low, until he felt fit enough for society again. When it came to anger, he knew what he was talking about. Yet dealing with Peter, he already felt in over his head.

He saw a flicker of something in Peter's gaze—maybe understanding, or firsthand experience grappling with fury. He'd also become more attentive.

"It's hard, man," Mark said. "Really hard. I get it."

"I'm never gonna stop being mad. I hate death!"

The statement made him think about Laurel and all she'd had to face alone. They had that in common. Since they'd met that morning, she'd popped into his head a dozen times, which worried him. He remembered how she didn't smile easily—but when she did, wow—and how cautious she seemed with him, insecure. Then the next thing he knew, she was spilling her life story over chocolate chip cookies.

Though she looked way too young to be a mother of a fourteen-year-old, she was still bound to be a bit older than Mark. Why was he even thinking this stuff? He wasn't going to get involved.

He liked her hopeful attitude, trusted her instincts about the B&B and decided she was nothing short of an inspiration the way she refused to let loss and grief—

being a widow, a single mother of three kids and over-loaded with responsibility—drag her down. Not to mention how tough it must be dealing with a hurting and grieving teen like Peter.

Ah, hell, he already was involved. The kid was still staring at him.

"You have a right to your anger, but your mom isn't the one who deserves it." Mark glanced up to see a perfect-sized swell for a newcomer. He jumped off the board, leaving Peter on his own. "Okay, catch this one. Paddle. Paddle. Paddle!"

And Peter paddled as if his life depended on it. Mark bodysurfed alongside him, keeping up as best he could as Peter first attempted a time or two to stand, then finally got up on one knee, stood for the blink of an eye, then fell off. When he resurfaced, Mark met him with a smile and praise.

"Hey, that was the best you've done yet!"

Surprisingly, considering the topic they'd just been tossing around, Peter smiled, too. "I'm starting to get the hang of it."

"Then you'll just have to keep taking lessons until you've got it."

"Can we catch one more?"

"That's the spirit."

An hour and a half later, the wind picked up and Peter was visibly chilled—his skin was pink-and-white blotchy to prove it—yet he didn't complain, just kept trying to stand up on the surfboard. He'd come close a couple of times, but never quite pulled everything together. Still he never gave up. Mark discovered he liked something about Peter—he wasn't a quitter.

"Lie down and I'll push you in," Mark said, treading water beside Peter and the surfboard.

For the second time that day, Peter didn't argue.

As he swam closer to shore, with the help of a wave pushing them the rest of the way, Mark wanted to ask a favor of Peter while he still had him on his turf. "When we get back, tell your mom you're sorry. She loves you, and it's got to hurt when you treat her like that."

Peter's lips curled inward as he put on his flip-flops and covered up with his father's Bart Simpson T-shirt. "Okay," he mumbled, reluctantly.

At 5:55 p.m., they walked back to where Main Street curved into the cul-de-sac, the B&B on one side, The Drumcliffe hotel on the other. Like Grandda always said, they really did own a little piece of heaven. "Good first lesson. I'll see you tomorrow at four for the next, okay?"

Peter nodded, seriously tired, but still interested.

"And start those exercises I showed you."

"Okay. My legs are kind of sore, though."

Mark grinned, leaving the kid at his front gate. "Get used to it. Later, man."

Peter smiled. "Later."

"I've been worried sick about you!" Laurel said from the porch.

"I was surfing with Mark." He rushed by her and toward the house like he hung out with Mark all the time.

"Mark?" He turned, and there was a near-shocked expression on her face. "Thank you."

"No problem."

Maybe Peter was saving the apology for dinner.

Tuesday, when Mark delivered Peter back to the B&B after his second surf lesson, Laurel was waiting.

"Will you join us for dinner?"

Did he want to do that? After spending his morning

finishing up painting the hotel trim, then working more on building the arbor, truth was, this was the most appealing offer he'd had all day. "Sure, what time?"

"Forty-five minutes?"

"Sounds good. Thanks." His spirits lifted by the invitation, Mark was struck that Laurel was the first woman he'd been drawn to since coming home to Sandpiper Beach.

A widow with three kids. Seriously, Delaney?

"One time I was on a fwing an—an a pider came an—an—an, I queemed!" Gracie said an hour later, as the girls took Mark on a tour of their living quarters. She must have felt obligated to entertain him while Laurel put the finishing touches on their meal. The unusual speech pattern was sweet, and knowing the history of her ear problems from Laurel yesterday—thinking she'd fallen down on the Mom-job—made him feel protective of both girls. And Laurel. He couldn't forget Peter, either. He wasn't sure what to make of that protective feeling, but he wouldn't deny it. Though it did make him uneasy.

"I fell off a swing once." Claire jumped in with a long and drawn-out story about exactly how her accident happened, the injuries she'd obtained, how her mother had cleaned her up, and on and on and on, while they walked down the hall toward their family room. Since he was the guest, for the sake of the little girls, he did his best to appear fascinated.

During the never-ending story, he also managed to assess the Prescott family living situation. The kitchen and in-dining breakfast area, downstairs bathroom and apparent three bedrooms with a medium-sized study, which they'd turned into their family room, was the

section of the grand old home where they lived. About
the size of a medium apartment. Unlike the foyer, the
front sitting room and the dining room, or the six upstairs bedrooms, it was furnished with modern, wear-
and-tear-styled furniture, which made sense with the
kids. Laurel Prescott knew how to be practical.

"And this is my mommy's room," Claire said. "She
has her own bathroom, but we all have to share that
one." She first gestured to the largest of the three bedrooms, probably once meant for the staff when the house
was built. Or an in-law suite? He glimpsed a humble
room with a comfortable-looking bed with tall bedposts
reminding him of her flair for antiques, and immediately felt like he'd invaded her privacy. Would she want
him gawking at her room? Then Claire pointed across
the hall to the main bathroom, and he was grateful for
the distraction. The main bathroom was spacious and
still had, what looked like, original tile in small white
hexagon shapes. The pedestal sink and bear-claw tub
also looked original, though the shower curtain encir-
cling it was covered with colorful safari animals. Yeah,
he bet Peter liked that, all right.

"We share, but Petie gwipes," Gracie added.

"That's Petie's room," Claire continued by pointing
to a closed door toward the end of the hall.

Since he'd arrived ten minutes ago, he hadn't seen
"Petie," but Mark had new understanding for why the
kid shut himself off.

The girls saved what they felt was the best for last.
Their room. Pink! White! Blindingly so. Frilly little
girl stuff throughout. Putting him completely out of
his comfort zone.

"Dinner's ready," Laurel called out. Thank God!

"Come on, awah-bubby! Dinner," Gracie said, taking off first.

"She means *everybody*," Claire quietly clarified, then made a beeline for their family dining room in the kitchen alcove.

Mark made a point to knock twice on Peter's closed door. "Dinner's ready." Just in case he hadn't heard his mother's announcement. Then he followed the girls.

Laurel looked great in tan capris and a pale blue tunic top, which brought out her hazel eyes. Maybe the touch of eye makeup she'd put on helped with that, too. Had she done that for him? He smiled, glad he'd combed his hair and dressed a little nicer than usual, wearing one of his best T-shirts, then waited for her to sit first. She looked a little nervous, so he didn't linger on her eyes, instead casting his gaze down to her sandals and noticing her tangerine-colored polish. Yeah, definitely in over his head. He never should have accepted her invitation.

Peter clumped down the hall, his feet seeming far too large for those skinny legs. Before he sat, he acknowledged Mark with a nod and partial smile. Then Claire insisted on saying a quick grace.

"I should say it. I'm Gwacie!"

"I said it first," and out went Claire's tongue.

"Now, girls."

Like so many family dinners at his own house, soon the plates were passed and the chaos began.

Mark wasn't used to being around kids, especially the chatty Claire and her little echo Gracie. He figured Laurel rarely got a quiet moment with them in the house. At least Peter's mood had lightened some since yesterday. His second lesson had gone about the same as the first, but Mark made sure he understood that everything worth learning took time.

Peter let his mom know she'd made his favorite—turkey meat loaf. Mark could tell by Laurel's surprised and pleased expression a compliment from the kid wasn't routine. She'd rounded out the meal with small baked potatoes, with several choices for toppings, and fresh green beans that smelled great thanks to lemon slices and a large sprig of rosemary cooked with them.

Conversation around the table had more to do with bargaining over how much each twin had to eat in order to call it dinner, and whether or not Peter had homework and had he done it yet, than getting-to-know-the-neighbor gab.

It brought back a slew of memories for Mark, of him and his brothers when they were young kids, squirming and trying to behave. And later when they'd all become touchy teens, ready to pounce on each other at the drop of one wrong word, or unwanted glance.

Other than Mark occasionally catching Laurel's gaze, and a special zing that took him by surprise whenever he did, they weren't able to communicate much at all. He was okay with that, since his goal was to keep the distance.

"So tell us about your surfing lessons, Peter," Laurel asked.

The kid said just enough words to qualify for an answer, then shoved more meat into his mouth. He seemed to have a healthy appetite, and Mark assumed it was from the beating he'd taken in the ocean that afternoon.

"Have you been doing those exercises I told you about?"

"Some." More eating, this time potato. "I'm gonna do more later."

"After your homework, right?" Laurel added between bites.

"Can we be excused?" the twins said in unison.

Laurel made a big deal out of checking their plates to make sure they'd eaten enough. "One more bite each."

They both crammed another tiny bite into their mouths, washed it down with the last of their milk and rushed off for the family room.

Peter had to be asked to clear the table, but he didn't protest too loudly, which surprised Mark. Maybe he wasn't such a problem all the time after all. Or maybe that was Peter on good behavior because of Mark being there.

Mark wanted to help, too, but Laurel wouldn't let him. "I'll clean up later. While the girls watch their TV show and Peter finishes his homework, I thought we could have some coffee or whatever you'd like to drink in the front sitting room."

An invitation for time alone? No matter how complicated the Prescott family's situation was, Mark couldn't resist the chance to get to know Laurel a little better. "Sure. Coffee's fine."

"I'll meet you in there," she said.

So he meandered into the front of the house. Rather than sit on the pillowed-out and overstuffed couch, or the matching ornate curved armchair beside it, he chose the classic paisley upholstered straight-backed chair across from the sofa, and waited for Laurel.

After looking around the room, he glanced out the front window toward the decidedly vintage-styled Drumcliffe and smiled, a few more ideas for perking up the place popping into his head. He also thought about Laurel and how having a brooding teen must stress her out, especially while juggling the twins and the hundreds of duties of the B&B. And the place wasn't even open yet. And once it was, would it even support them? He wouldn't suppose her situation, but figured there was probably life insurance meeting some of their needs.

He wondered what profession her deceased husband was in.

Then stopped himself. Enough already.

She brought coffee on a tray, like they did in old movies, and he got a kick out of all the effort she'd gone to for him. But this was a B&B, and she was the proprietor. Of course she'd do this for the guests. In fact, she was probably practicing on him. That was all.

He poured cream into his coffee and soon enjoyed the hint of vanilla and cinnamon. If this was only practice, he was happy to be her guinea pig, because it made their sitting alone together in a fancy room feel less intimate.

"I wanted to personally thank you for your help these last two days. Peter told me what happened at the beach yesterday."

"No big deal. Those kids were up to no good."

"It *was* a big deal. Who knows what would've happened if you hadn't shown up."

"Well, I did, and Peter got some surfing lessons out of it."

"I hope he keeps it up."

"He says he wants to."

She went quiet for a moment. "I never thought he'd get bullied simply for being the new kid in town."

"In a perfect world, it shouldn't make any difference, but…"

She primly sipped her coffee from a pink patterned cup that probably came from England. The one inside the box he'd first carried yesterday?

He didn't want to, but couldn't help noticing her

mouth, how the top lip was slightly plumper than the bottom. Rather than get caught staring again, he took in how tonight her hair was tamed with a conservative hair band, and how she looked like a proper bed-and-breakfast owner. Then he glanced down at her bright tangerine toenails, enjoying the contradiction.

She caught him staring, too, and he didn't even try to look away. Why pretend when he liked what he saw? So he smiled, and judging by the twitch at one corner of her mouth, she didn't mind.

"So what are you going to call this place?"

"The Prescott Bed-and-Breakfast. I've got a sign, just haven't put it up yet."

"I can do it."

"Would you?"

On impulse, he decided he might just help out from time to time. She was a widow with three kids and needed all the help she could get. Not because he found her attractive, and she interested him, and he felt good around her. But as backup. Only to help her out, as a handyman, because she could use it. That was the main reason.

Right. And Grandda didn't believe in selkies.

"Sure. The sooner you start to advertise the better."

"Tomorrow, then?"

He refilled his coffee. "Absolutely."

For now, he'd buy the little white lie about helping her out because she needed it. Otherwise he might get uptight about making another excuse to see her tomorrow, and he didn't want to be tense when having her all to himself in the sitting room right now felt so right.

Laurel sipped coffee and watched Mark's big hands as he grappled with the teapot made for ladies. She hid her smile behind the antique china cup. He'd obviously ogled her pedicure, and she wondered if there was anything else he might like about her. It had been a long time since she'd seen appreciative gazes from a man, and, being honest, she'd missed it.

Was that why she kept asking him to come back?

Or was it because, beyond his all-man appearance, he was nice? He'd intervened on her son's behalf. He was a man and her boy needed male mentoring? Lord only knew she was out of her depth on that one. She hadn't a clue that Peter, gangly and new in town, would be the subject of teasing. From what Peter had said, the teasing had been heading in a much more serious direction when Mark showed up.

What kind of mother was she? One who seriously needed to make time to read some books on parenting teens. Maybe if he was more confident, hadn't been devastated by losing his father…

Her mind drifted back to the present. Instead of required reading, she was sitting in the parlor with a man who emitted more sex appeal than the last three seasons of bachelors combined. Did he have a clue?

Yesterday he'd hinted at needing a life coach as much as she did, so that was something they had in common. With his time in the Middle East, and her husband's losing battle with cancer, they'd both been through hell. There was one other, more positive thing they had in common, too: they'd both been raised in a small beach town.

She could hear him swallow. Deep in thought, it'd grown too quiet. "So tell me about the history of The Drumcliffe."

An easy subject to tackle, he did so with ease, giving her the story from all the way back when his grandfather came from Ireland. As he spoke, she enjoyed the sparkle in his blue eyes, darkened by the parlor lighting, and how tiny the teacup looked in his hands. His lower lip curled out the tiniest bit, and she wondered how it would feel to kiss him.

What? She took another sip of her coffee. Maybe she *was* ready to…

Oh, the mere thought made her stomach knot and a hope chest of guilt crash over her shoulders. But there he was, sharing his family's story, natural as could be, smiling with pride. What could be wrong with a little longing?

She took another sip, admiring every aspect of Mark Delaney. She'd caught him checking her out earlier, and knew how that felt. Good, by the way. Now the tables were turned, but she didn't want to give the wrong impression, and the last thing she needed was to get caught. Taking yet another sip of her cooling coffee, she wondered how long she could hide behind her teacup before being obvious.

Chapter Three

"Hey, Peter, give me a hand," Mark said that Wednesday afternoon, as he prepared to sink the white posts for the brand-spanking-new Prescott Bed-and-Breakfast sign.

The teen sat on the front porch playing a handheld video game and didn't bother to look up.

So he made his loud tooth whistle. "Dude!"

Finally, Peter's head bobbed up.

"Come help." It wasn't a question.

"I don't know how."

"So you'll learn."

Reluctantly, Peter put down his device and padded in his flip-flops across the grass toward Mark. "Like I said, I don't know how to do this stuff, and we're supposed to have another surf lesson."

"We'll make up for that tomorrow." He watched the kid hide his disappointment. "I promise."

That got a better response.

"Okay, here's what we're going to do."

Over the next hour Mark showed Peter how to dig a hole, set an anchor, use an electric drill—which he especially liked—place washers and install a nut. Peter had obviously never so much as hammered a nail, but the how-to approach seemed to capture his interest enough. At least he tried.

"See that pile of wood over there?" Mark pointed to the grassy yard across the road, between the hotel and the beach.

"Yeah?"

"That's going to be a gazebo, and I want you to help me build it this weekend."

"Me!" The kid's voice cracked and his eyes nearly bugged out.

"Yeah, you need experience hammering nails, and I can teach you how to use more power tools, a cross-cut saw, table and band saw, you name it. What do you say?"

"Why?"

"Because knowing how to do a few useful things will build your confidence." Which he needed. *And will come in handy for your mother, too.* "Like learning how to surf."

"What if I don't want to?"

"Surf?"

"No. Help."

Not an option. Think fast. "Think of it this way. Our hotel is right on Main Street, the biggest road that leads straight to the beach." He glanced up the road lined with palm and fruitless olive trees, small local businesses, storefronts and, in the distance on a hill, the local high school. "All the girls come this way to the beach, and they'll see you building stuff. They'll notice you. Might open some doors."

Peter stood staring across the street at the pile of wood, then glanced up toward what passed as the town center, small as it was.

"It's better than babysitting your sisters, isn't it?" Mark noticed the click in his expression from on-the-fence to makes-perfect-sense. Whether it was the girls or not dealing with his sisters, Mark had sold him on the proposition, and though the last thing he needed was a novice assistant, he wanted to help the kid. Maybe he'd find out something new about himself, feel better and, like he'd said, be more confident. Or, he could smash his finger with a hammer, get the mother of all splinters and never want to go near wood again. It was a gamble, but worth the risk.

A half hour later, after a few finishing touches on the posts, and with plans to meet Saturday morning to begin building, they'd hung the B&B sign.

"It's beautiful!" Laurel called from the porch, her eyes bright with excitement. It was obvious she'd made a conscious effort not to hover over her son while he helped Mark, but from a safe distance she'd followed the whole process. "I've got to take a picture." She whipped out her phone and rushed down the yard toward them.

"You get in it, and I'll take the picture," Mark offered.

"Oh." Her hand flew to her hair. "I wasn't planning on—"

"You look fine. I'll get a few shots and you can choose the best one, then put it on Facebook."

"I'm not crazy about social media."

"But you've got to create a buzz."

"You've got a point." She glanced at her son. "Peter,

you worked so hard on this, come be in the picture with me?" she said with pride.

"Ah, Mom." He obviously didn't want anything to do with smiling for a camera, but he hadn't wanted to help sink the posts, either, and there they were.

"We want to!" Claire came rushing through the screen door and down the porch steps wearing plastic play heels, clicking all the way, Gracie hot on her tail clack, clack, clacking. Laurel split them up, putting one on each side of the sign.

After some arm-twisting, Mark managed to get a picture of the entire family, with a good portion of the beautiful house behind them. He had to admit, Laurel's smile was captivating, and he thought about secretly sending a copy of one shot in particular to his email. It was of her alone, of course, looking proud, maybe a little nervous but alluring, as she often did. Her understated confidence was just one of the things he liked about her.

"This is the best picture. Agree?"

She shrugged, but he could tell she liked it, too. *Yeah, that one, definitely that one.* "Should I post it?"

"Sure."

It was time to face the fact. His grandfather had a word for it—*smitten.* Mark would never use that term, but he needed to admit he dug her. Yup. There. He'd finally allowed himself to think it. He liked her, and not just in a pure neighborly sort of way. Ready or not. Maybe he'd blame it on the tangerine pedicure.

"There you go." He handed her the phone. "Anything you want to say with the picture?"

"Oh, sure." Her thumbs flew over the phone, and Mark took the opportunity to watch her up close. Yeah, as bad of an idea as it was, he liked her all right.

* * *

Laurel finally realized, with Mark's hinting, she was behind in the social media game. Instead of going all ditzy over an appealing man like she'd been doing since he'd helped her that first day, she needed to hunker down and finalize her plan for opening the B&B. Sure, she'd given it a lot of thought before she'd bought the place, but making the move and starting the kids in new schools all at the same time had taken her eye off the prize.

She had catching up to do and plans to firm up. Ads to run in the tricounty local papers, visits to make to the chamber of commerce.

What about a mock run? She could invite three local travel agents to spend the night as a sort of rehearsal, maybe get some good endorsements in the process. Her head spun with new ideas, thanks to Mark's gentle nudging, and she needed to get back on her game, instead of ogling her sexy neighbor. Pronto.

On Thursday afternoon, Peter finally stood on his own for a short ride during their surfing lesson, and the kid beamed all the way on the walk home. On the porch, Laurel lifted a brow when her son gave her a hug on his way into the house. Progress.

"He had a good day at the beach," Mark said. "I'll let him tell you about it."

She lifted her shoulders as if she'd just seen magic. "That's great." Her earnest glance kept him from rushing off, that and how her hair lifted with the afternoon breeze.

She ventured down the stairs—he couldn't take his eyes off her—and met him at the gate. "Can I borrow you tomorrow night?"

The request put all kinds of thoughts in his head.

"I'm putting together a few appetizers I plan to serve in the evenings along with wine for the guests." With her head tipped, she hopefully glanced up. "I need a taster."

Looking bashful, like a young girl, she'd used words like borrow and taste, and had thrown him. "Me?" His delayed response. "I should put you in touch with Rita, our restaurant chef. Get her opinion. Or my mom, she'd be great for this."

"But I want you." Her fingers lightly grazed his forearm.

Want me? When was the last time he'd heard a woman say that? "What time?" he said, far too aware of her touch.

"Seven. Be sure to save up your appetite." Her sweet smile, and twinkling eyes made the hair on his neck salute.

Liking the way she'd made him feel, he let go a slow smile, and they spent a long moment looking in each other's eyes. "See you then."

Friday evening, after a long day of construction work on the early stages of the gazebo, and yet another surfing lesson with Peter, Mark took extra time to clean up good. He'd shaved off his usual two-day growth, even slapped on for the first time the woodsy aftershave his mother had given him last Christmas. *Sniff, sniff.* Too much? He stepped out of the bathroom.

Conor sprawled on the couch in the sitting room of their shared hotel suite watching the local news. Yup, they were two grown men still living at home. Well, at the family hotel, anyway. It used to be even more cramped when Daniel lived there, too, while starting up his physical medicine clinic. No wonder Grandda was hell-bent they'd each be finding the love of their life soon, just to get them out of the fold. *Remember the selkie!* The phrase was beginning to sound like a T-shirt slogan.

Daniel had met and married Keela, so chalk one up for Grandda. Conor had a good excuse for still living at home, though. He was saving all his money for the down payment on a house he'd wanted since he was a kid. The Beacham house was abandoned, forgotten and falling apart, and sat hauntingly along the cliffs on the outskirts of town. Whereas Mark still lived here because he had nowhere else to go while getting back on his feet.

The family offer was clearly on the table—take over the hotel—but he still wasn't sure if he wanted the responsibility of running the entire family business. His parents thought he could do it, but what if he failed, ruining decades of their hard work? Three generations could go down the drain. It occurred to him, while he was so bent on helping Peter develop some confidence, maybe he should start working on himself, too.

"Man, you smell like you mean business," Conor said the minute Mark stepped out of the bathroom, naked except for the towel around his waist.

"Good or bad?"

"If I say I like it, will you think less of me?" The tallest though youngest of the three brothers, Conor, who looked more like a professional athlete than a sheriff, grinned.

Mark smirked. "Can I borrow a shirt?"

"Okay, now I'm curious." Conor muted the TV. "What's up?"

"Just helping out the lady across the street."

"You mean the good-looking brunette?"

Mark stopped riffling through Conor's abundant collection of shirts.

"Think I hadn't noticed?"

He met his brother's knowing gaze for the first time.

"And she's got three kids."

Mark opted to pass over that reminder, for another fact. "I figure she's around thirty-five."

"A cougar," Conor teased. "All *riight*."

"Her? Hardly. Besides that's only four years' difference. We're just feeling each other out." He did his best to sound nonchalant, though inwardly grimacing over his word choice.

Conor's brows shot up. "Sounds promising."

Mark gave an ironic laugh and chose a smoky-blue button-down shirt from his brother's closet, then tried it on. "What about this one?"

Conor went overboard standing, assessing, rubbing his chin with his fingers while walking around him. "It brings out your eyes," he said doing an obvious imitation of the male fashion consultant from that runway reality show.

Mark unwrapped the bath towel, twirled it tight, then snapped it at his brother.

Jumping aside, Conor grinned. "I dare you to show up like that," he said, making note of Mark being completely naked from the waist down. "Make one helluva first-date impression."

Laurel fed her kids an early dinner and set the girls up playing Candy Land and building a new Legos kit. Peter was always happy to be left alone, especially after another surfing lesson from Mark. She liked how Mark had made the effort to get Peter engaged in the B&B

sign hanging yesterday, too. Once again reinforcing the boy really needed a man's influence.

She finished making half a dozen different appetizers, hoping Mark would help her decide the top three for the B&B opening. She uncorked the red wine—a silky mixture of three different grapes—to let it breathe and next opened an unoaked white, pushing it into the ice bucket to keep the crisp wine chilled. Then she went to the dining room and carefully laid classic china plates and linen napkins on the antique oak buffet.

Why were her fingers trembling? Was she that nervous about the mock run she'd planned for next week, and opening the B&B for business after that? Or did the tall and intriguing Mark Delaney with great abs have something to do with her jitters?

No-brainer.

The doorbell rang and she rushed to answer it, and what was on the other side nearly took her breath away. She'd already made the mistake of noticing Mark's sexy mouth, so now as it stretched slowly into a relaxed smile, she couldn't avoid the gorgeous spectacle. Because he'd shaved, and there was nothing like a man's smooth face to make a woman want to run her hand along his jaw. Her eyes widened and she looked away…to his eyes.

Beneath his brows, those deep-set blue eyes stood out like they never had before. Maybe it was the time of day, or the shirt—which was a definite good choice.

"Hi," he said. "Too early?"

Scrambling to cover how flustered he'd suddenly made her feel, she swallowed and forced a welcoming grin. "No. Not at all." She invited him in, noticing a catchy masculine fragrance, and liked it, then started immediately toward the back of the house. "I've got the appetizers lined up in the kitchen. Just gotta move them to the dining room, where they'll actually be if I ever get guests."

"You mean when. *When* you get guests."

"Oh, right. Positive thinking." Why did sensing him right behind her make her edgy? Was it the fact he smelled so great? Or looked so handsome, in a natural all-guy kind of way. He was younger than her—she couldn't forget that little zinger.

"Whatever's easiest for you," he said, watching her oddly, like he'd totally caught on how he made her feel.

Could he tell? "Well, the ambiance is nicer in there."

Without being asked, he stepped up and carried two of the platters to the dining room. "Wow, these look great."

"Thanks." She brought two others, then they made one final trip together for the last two platters and the wine. *Focus on why you invited him, not how great he looks. Or smells.* "I plan on rotating the appetizers for those who stay more than one night."

"Makes sense." He stopped, his hands on his hips in a total guy way. "So you want to pretend I'm a guest?" A mischievous smile creased those inviting lips, and she went all skittish again. It'd been far too long since she'd been in the company of an attractive man. Since Alan's death, she'd never even missed it until she'd noticed Mark Delaney across the street five days ago. A quick pang of sadness and loss settled in her chest. Reminding her of what she'd been through and how much she'd lost. She took a breath. All she had to do was focus on Mark's pretending to be a guest.

"Oh, well, okay." She gestured for him to sit.

"Wait," he said. "Have you taken a picture and uploaded it to your social media pages?"

Why hadn't she thought of that? Because she'd been too distracted by him. "No. Another great idea." She went back into the kitchen to retrieve her cell phone, then snapped a couple of pictures and got Mark's approval for the best one to share. The one with the two wine bottles in the background. He took her phone and used his thumbs superfast, then showed her what he'd written.

Appetizers at five. Join us? Prescott B&B, Sandpiper Beach. Opening soon.

"You've got a real knack for this sort of thing."

"Mom needed some help getting The Drumcliffe online. I had to take a crash course on the whole social media thing. Even figured out how to upload a virtual tour on our website."

"Impressive. You're a natural."

"We could do one for the B&B, too," he said.

"I'd love it!"

He smiled like he was as excited for her opening as she was, which touched her. She gestured for him to sit again. "I plan to show every guest around when they check in. Mind if I practice my talk on you?"

"Not at all."

"Oh, and don't wait for me, start eating."

He sat and looked at everything, but did wait while she recited a little welcome speech she'd worked up, feeling more like a child in school instead of a thirty-five-year-old woman. As she did, she poured him a small glass of each wine. To help him decide, she placed before him the cheese platter with honey, fig spread and assorted nuts. On the second plate was crostini with three different homemade toppings to choose from— guacamole, mashed minted peas and salsa. The third item was pinwheels made from feta and cream cheese with dried cranberries in flour tortillas, then came the stuffed mushrooms, and finally the sweet-and-sour meatballs on one plate and tiny crab cakes on another. She'd labeled each plate since her guests would self-serve at their leisure between 5:00 and 6:00 p.m. each evening.

"Wow," was all Mark said, but looking deep in thought.

"Be honest, okay? Rate them favorite to least."

"Aren't you going to join me?"

She sat next to him, poured herself a small glass of red wine and spread some Brie with honey and fig on a cracker. "Sure. It's no fun to eat alone." Though occasionally she longed for the luxury of eating by herself, without a single kid needing her attention.

"Don't I know that." He appeared to be having trouble choosing which appetizer to have first.

Did he eat alone a lot? Could a person be lonely living and working at a family hotel like The Drumcliffe? She'd assumed otherwise, but his reply had told her different.

"Damn, I feel like I've died and gone to mini-buffet heaven," he said, smiling as he popped a meatball into his mouth. "Oh, that's good."

"Have as much of everything as you want." His general reaction to her efforts and to her invitation warmed her on the inside in a way she hadn't felt in two years.

Then she realized how much she'd missed being around a man, and Mark Delaney was the reason. Just as quickly, that pang of fear returned.

Mark had eaten until he was full, enjoying every bite. Having a glass of wine, something he didn't do very often, had also mellowed him out. He wondered why The Drumcliffe didn't do something similar as a perk for their guests. They put carafes of coffee out every morning in the lobby, so why not add something like this in the evening? It wouldn't need to be as special as this, but something. Maybe Grandda could offer house wine and draft beer in the pub for their guests for a couple of hours each evening, too. Guests only, though, or the locals would flood the pub if word got out. The flowing ideas were all food for thought, along with Laurel's amazing appetizers.

She looked great, too. Her hair was down, and she'd put on lipstick. For him? Could a woman like her be the least bit interested in a guy like him? A handyman working for his parents? *Don't flatter yourself, buddy.* This was nothing more than practice for future guests. Of course she'd dress up. He tried to convince himself he played zero part in the reason she looked so nice right then, but part of him—a long-forgotten part— wanted to think she might be attracted to him, too. He hoped so, anyway.

What was it about Laurel that made him wish things could be different, and want things again?

She wore a yellow summer sweater set with a knee-length, straight khaki skirt, affording him the best view of her legs yet. Narrow ankles, nice calves, smooth-looking skin. And thanks to her choice in sandals, he got another glimpse of those tangerine-colored toenails. He liked everything he saw, and most of all was glad he was here with her.

He took another drink of the wine, she'd done the same, and their gazes overlapped midsip, causing a tiny pop of adrenalin in his chest. Her hazel-brown eyes were warm and rich like the silky taste of the three-grape blended red, and they watched him thoughtfully.

Hopefully she wasn't a mind reader, because he was still all kinds of messed up from his stint in the military. Part of him wanted to slide right into something nice with her, another part unsure and reluctant to try. But staring into those gorgeous eyes, he wanted to.

"Hey, can I have a meatball?" Peter appeared, hair disheveled like he'd just woken up.

"Of course." Laurel quickly snapped out of their invigorating staring contest, which disappointed Mark, even though he understood she couldn't continue making doe eyes at him in front of her son.

"Can we have some?"

"Can we have some?"

The twins had arrived. Laurel handed them each a cranberry and cream cheese pinwheel.

The boy wolfed down the last three meatballs before hitting the guacamole and toast.

He seemed in a good enough mood, so on a whim, Mark decided to take advantage of the situation.

"Peter, will you watch the girls for a little while so your mother and I can take a walk on the beach?"

Midchew, Peter looked confused, probably wondering why Mark would want to hang out with his mother.

"Play game-ios with us?" Gracie pleaded.

Peter screwed up his face. "I'll watch TV with you, but I get to choose," he bargained. "And I'm taking the guacamole with me." He gathered up the plate, and without giving a definitive answer, walked down the hall with his sisters.

"I guess that's a yes," Laurel said, looking happy.

As they started out the door, Laurel called back into the house. "Be good. I'll be back in a while."

"Okay," Peter called out, apparently unfazed by his

involuntary assignment. At least he was inside. Nobody from school would see him.

"Okay!" Claire.

"Oh. Kay!" Gracie.

They stepped off the porch into cool night air and a clear sky, a bit too early for most of the stars to show.

"Since you've started giving Peter surfing lessons, he seems a little happier. Doesn't brood as much. Well, maybe *happy* isn't the right word for it, but...*calmer*? Anyway, I've noticed he's not giving me as much attitude as usual."

"Seriously?"

"Yes, and I have to thank you for that."

He wasn't at all sure he deserved the credit, but he liked the expression on her face as they headed for the beach, so he smiled back. Maybe he was a good influence.

"Definite progress. He doesn't resent every single thing I say to him, only a few." She laughed and took off her sandals to walk barefoot in the still-warm sand. "He's lightened up with his sisters, too."

Mark kept quiet, enjoying her carefree conversation. If she wanted to attribute the kid's attitude adjustment to him, fine, but the only payment he needed was seeing the lack of stress on her beautiful face.

And yes, he'd just secretly admitted he thought she was beautiful.

If he continued to keep connecting with Peter, maybe he'd earn the kid's trust. Did he want the responsibility of that, though? Mark let go of the uncertain thought, focusing instead on Laurel and her shapely legs walking ahead of him toward the waves. In the moment, attraction overruled concern. He lengthened his stride and caught up.

"We're not in a hurry, are we?" he asked.

"Oh. No. I'm so used to rushing through everything, I guess I've forgotten how to relax."

Crazy thought, but he wanted to teach her how. Maybe it would help him remember, too. He took her hand, which she didn't fight, and set a slower pace. "Take a deep breath. Enjoy yourself for a change." Her thin fingers were cool, though her palm felt warm against his, and it was great to hold a woman's hand again.

She did as he suggested, slowing down to a stroll, inhaling the ocean air, then a few steps later she looked at him with a questioning gaze. "Is that how I come off? Uptight all the time?"

She hadn't said it defensively, or as a challenge, just a query, so he gave her his honest opinion. "You've got a lot of responsibilities, and let's just say, sometimes I can tell you're struggling."

She went silent as they walked past the lifeguard station, toward a long stretch of beach. A minute later she squeezed his hand. "I've probably taken on more than I should've, but we needed a new start." She checked him out, as though wondering if it was okay to talk about her past. He sent an encouraging glance. "It was so sad at our old house, all the memories, the gaping hole Alan had left by dying. He'd written me a note telling me to do something special with his second life insurance policy. It took close to two years to decide, but I finally did. Now, most days I think I'm crazy."

"I think it's great you bought that place. The house is gorgeous." *So are you.* "Everything you've done is amazing." He stopped to look at her before saying his next thought. "I know how it is to focus so hard on something that all the rest fades away. As a person who may have forgotten how to enjoy myself, too, I'm just saying."

"Takes one to know one?"

He smiled and nodded, enjoying how the moonlight sparkled in her eyes. How she suddenly looked impish.

She pushed him with both palms, then took off running for the damp sand, heading toward the ocean. "First one in wins!" She hiked up her skirt to her thighs so she could run faster. He definitely liked that.

Momentarily stunned by her sudden change, Mark stood still, then quickly responded to her challenge and ran after her.

She squealed when her feet hit the cold water. "I win!"

"That's just a toe dip. You said first one *in*." He rushed beside her, not giving a damn that his jeans were sopping wet up to his knees, and his cross-trainers pooled with water, and swooped her up into his arms, then pretended to throw her into the next wave.

She screamed and stiffened, then laughed, but screamed again as he pretended to hoist her into the waves, counting one, two, three! She buried her face on his shoulder, and he liked having her there, in his arms, laughing.

A fast-moving, receding wave pulled at the backs of his knees, and he lost his footing as the sand quickly got sucked from under his feet, nearly dropping her. Staggering back to a wide stance, refusing to let her go, he nearly recovered until a second wave rolled in, hitting faster and harder, and higher up. Drenching both of them. His jeans were sopping and heavy, now. And they didn't stand a chance. Down the two of them went into the cold pool of swirling ocean. He yelled and she screamed.

"I'm sorry!" he called, worried what she'd think of him, assuming she was ticked off. But she laughed hysterically, and once he helped her stand, she splashed him, then ran back to the wet sand and took off farther down the beach. What could he do but follow? Though running in drenched denim and soggy shoes was a definite challenge. Not to mention the chaffing.

"What'll the kids think when I come home like this?" she called over her shoulder.

"That you had some fun?"

Finally, he caught up. They were both out of breath, but she was still smiling, and he realized how much he liked Peter's mom. In fact, as he wrapped his arms around her and they smiled at each other up close—she cold and shivering—he understood exactly how much he liked her, enough to want to kiss her.

It'd been a long time since he'd been in a good enough place to even think about kissing a woman. He hadn't felt this drawn to someone since before his last deployment, two years ago.

But Mark and Laurel were just getting to know each other. If he followed through on this crazy whim and kissed her, wouldn't it mess up the friendly-neighbor bit? With three kids, she needed a helping hand more than a boyfriend.

From the shift in her playful expression to serious, he sensed she'd figured out exactly what'd just been going on in his mind. Yeah, he still wanted to kiss her. And where he'd hesitated, with a lift of her chin she seemed to dare him.

So he kissed her, cold, salty and wet, discovering soft, warm and inviting lips. That her pouty upper lip did indeed feel as good as it looked. The cautious kiss didn't take long, but it planted a warm, glad feeling in the center of his chest. Though Laurel gave a modest look when it ended, like they'd just broken a rule or something, she took his hand as they walked back to her house.

He liked holding her hand even more now, and wished he'd kissed her the way he'd really wanted.

When they got to her gate, sopping wet from the waist down, Mark opted not to go in. "You can tell them I dared you to go swimming."

"I was going to tell them I had to save you from a shark."

"Good one."

She looked relaxed all right, and playful, and he wondered what she'd be like, just the two of them in that big old house now that they'd broken the ice.

"Got anything for me to do tomorrow?"

She took her time answering, letting her gaze travel around him, a different kind of look in her eyes. Flirty. "Oh, I'm sure I'll come up with something." Then she turned and headed for her porch. "Before or after your project with Peter?" she said at the door.

"After."

"I'll make lunch."

"You don't have to do that."

"I want to."

"Okay, then, good."

"Good," she said, sounding sassy.

If he wasn't mistaken she'd just flat out flirted with him. He liked that. A lot. So he smiled to himself. As he walked back to his room, shoes squeaking, rubbing his heels, his cold, water-laden jeans dragging on the asphalt, and scraping the insides of his thighs, even with beach sand finding its way into strange places, he kept grinning. Tonight, spending one-on-one time with Laurel had been great, and with plans to see her again, tomorrow was already looking up.

Chapter Four

Saturday, after five long hours of manual labor with Mark as the foreman and Peter the journeyman apprentice, they'd managed good headway with the gazebo frame. Peter had learned how to use several new-to-him power tools, including table and band saws, plus, from the way he grinned every time he used it, his personal favorite, the nail gun.

Laurel made an appearance around 12:30 p.m. to remind them that lunch would be served at one. They worked across the street on the cul-de-sac yard abutting the side of The Drumcliffe. The rolling green lawn extended toward the beach, and was the perfect spot for the gazebo. She showed up wearing brown leggings, displaying her nice curves, and a sleeveless top, loose, but sexy, giving him a glimpse of her light olive skin and thin arms. Best of all, her hair was in a ponytail again. Mark was surprised how much he looked forward to lunch, too, so he rushed things along on the building front. They sunk the posts, braced the beams, even adding some windows in record time. In other words, they were more than ready for lunch when, a half hour later, Laurel called from her curb. What a spread she'd made, too. The kitchen island was covered in do-it-yourself sandwich fixings. Assorted meats and cheeses, three different breads, everything from lettuce to tomatoes and pickles.

"You may want to try that before you use it," Laurel said, pointing out a small bowl of something that looked like he'd want to spread it on bread. It sat next to the standard mayo and mustard jars.

Mark hadn't washed his hands yet, and Laurel dipped her index finger into the "secret sauce" and came at him.

"Taste this. Let me know what you think."

He stared for an instant at her proffered finger. A dozen inappropriate thoughts crossed his mind. Did she know what she was doing to him? Innocently, she waited for his tongue to appear, then served the tip of her finger, covered in spread, for his tasting pleasure. He went for it, savoring every sensation as it came along. Warm skin, spicy spread.

It happened so fast, he was stunned by how sexy licking her finger could be. He'd also made the mistake of looking her in the eyes when he did. Oh, yeah, this was more than tasting the spread, this was a continuation of that kiss they'd shared and took it to a whole new level. A dozen more thoughts blasted through his mind, causing his skin to heat up, and since they were in front of her kids, all crowding around the island to make their own versions of lunch, he fought off the urge to grab and kiss her.

She'd seen it, too. His flash of desire. Because she'd been watching. Teasing? Had she done that on purpose, that uber-sexy taste-my-finger bit?

The moment stretched on, and he realized she waited for his reaction, preferably something verbal, and definitely from above the belt.

"Wow," he said. "What'd you put in there?"

She dipped her head sideways, wearing a sweet, yet smug expression. "That's my little secret. Trust me." Oh, he wanted to. "Spread that on your bread and it'll make any meat pop."

Did she just say that? Right in front of the kids? He hadn't been this turned on discussing sandwiches since, well, *ever.*

"Definitely going to use that." He pointed at the innocent little bowl sitting on the counter, then went to wash his hands, thinking cold, cold water over the head would be more appropriate.

After lunch at the B&B, where his turkey definitely popped between the sheets—uh, he meant bread— Laurel, as promised, had found something for Mark to do.

She got out her laptop, opened it on the counter and, while the twins carried the dishes and utensils to the sink and she cleaned up, she had Peter display the big surprise.

A website for the B&B. She'd taken his advice, and that fact touched him nearly as much as tasting her finger.

"I uploaded a website for the Prescott B&B," Peter said. "It's just a basic theme, but Mom helped me pick some pictures and, well, what do you think?"

Besides the fact it was awfully late to just be doing this? "This is great." Mark was truly impressed, and glad to get his mind off Laurel and how she made him feel. "It doesn't look like you need my help with *anything*."

"Wasn't it your idea to include virtual tours?" Laurel reminded, from the sink area.

"Oh, yeah. This is the perfect place to post them."

"That's why I need your help." And there he was staring into those amazing eyes again. "You're the guy with the fancy-schmancy seven plus smartphone."

"Ah, right." So she'd wound him tight around her finger for a reason. But he preferred to think she'd been flat out flirting with him.

For the next hour, he and Laurel toured each of the six guest rooms using his phone video camera to film a slow 360-degree turn. They had to reshoot a couple of them because Mark had bumped into something by accident, or his hand wasn't steady enough. How could he be steady in bedroom after bedroom, with Laurel standing close enough to breathe on his neck?

After, he took a picture of each room from the best angle to post under the ROOMS heading on the website. Next, he went out front and filmed a walk up to the wraparound porch and entrance into the house. He got the bright idea to walk slowly up the inside stairwell to the second-floor landing, too. She'd done such a beautiful job of arranging the antique furniture there. The sitting area seemed to invite guests to try out the chairs and love seats, to linger and enjoy reading a book from the well-stocked built-in bookcases. She must have spent a lot of time in used bookstores to find most of the leather-bound classics, though she also had a wide assortment of current paperbacks. When all the filming was done, he sent the videos to Peter to upload on the new website.

These were the only moments he had alone with Laurel, and it was strictly business. Sure, they'd accidentally bumped into each other while filming several times, followed by exaggerated "excuse mes" and "no problems," but that wasn't the quality time he'd been hoping for. Just her and him, alone, in her pretty house. Maybe another day.

He still enjoyed himself, because it was time spent with Laurel. What had gotten into him? He was still fighting the idea of taking over the hotel. Why the sudden desire to get involved? With a woman who came complete with a family, no less.

After Peter completed the website, Laurel, the twins and Mark watched Peter as he clicked the various pages, conducted each virtual room tour and signed up for the Prescott B&B newsletter. They all cheered and high-fived like they'd invented a rocket set for outer space.

"Time for cookies!" Laurel announced. The twins jumped up and down, and Mark smiled.

While Peter chowed down several cookies, Mark went through the website again, comparing it with The Drumcliffe Hotel's online presence.

"Your online reservation link isn't hooked up with anything," Mark noted.

"What do you mean?" Laurel looked concerned, maybe uptight?

"To other programs that give you more visibility. But we can fix that. Let me give my dad a call." As predicted, Sean promptly picked up. "Dad, can you come across the street for a minute? We need your help." Mark liked how "we" sounded, like he belonged somewhere besides with his family.

In the time it took Mark to eat a cookie, his father's shadow loomed over the Victorian's front door. Mark let him in, then made introductions as Sean Delaney appraised the first floor of the B&B.

Laurel's eyes darted between father and son, his father being a full three inches taller than Mark. He may look imposing, but the former high school math and history teacher was nothing short of a gentle giant. Unless you ticked him off, then look out.

Mark escorted him to the kitchen and made introductions. Laurel offered him a cookie, which he partook of, then he sat on a stool and, wasting no time, walked Laurel through the various options for small business owners like her.

"I get the need for this, but call me old school, or out of it, but whatever happened to people calling or emailing for reservations?"

"I used to feel the same way," Sean said, reassuringly, looking like the biggest man in the room—because he was. "But let me show you a few things."

With his reading glasses perched on the end of his nose, he surfed the web. "There are programs you can download, or services you can sign up for. See this?" He pointed to the screen and Laurel moved in closer. "This is a website reservation group you sign up for and pay a small monthly fee that offers alternative distribution systems, shows availability, and most importantly, gets you greater visibility. See, it even breaks down the price per number for rooms you have to rent. How many do you have?"

"Six." Wrapped up in the moment, Mark jumped in, answering for Laurel. She didn't seem to mind.

"Okay, so for less than twenty bucks a month they can provide all of these services." He leaned back and gave her time and space to read what they offered.

"There are also cloud based reservations software programs, but I kind of like this one."

"So this website reservations program can show my openings on bigger sites, like my local chamber of commerce?"

"Exactly, more exposure."

"You don't have to sign up for this if you don't feel ready," Mark added, wanting to offer Laurel support on whatever decision she made. Laurel looked relieved when she glanced at him.

"So there's no overlapped bookings?"

"Nope," Sean said. "If someone signs up through them it goes automatically to your calendar."

Sean pointed to another section of the computer screen. "See, they offer a free trial, if you want I can sign you up and you can see if this works for you or not. If you don't like it, just cancel."

"Thank you, Mr. Delaney."

"Call me Sean."

"Okay, Sean. If you don't mind, I'm going to think about this, and if you could bookmark this web link for me, I'll know where to go to sign up for the free trial. I can afford a small fee per month, I guess, if it does what it says, and I like the services."

"They've got a good rating, so no problem there." Sean glanced at Laurel, then Mark. Like a gentleman, never pushing a point, Sean nodded and accepted her resistance. "If you decide, any way I can help, just let me know. By the way, you've done a great job with this old house. Looks fantastic."

"Thank you."

Mark liked how Laurel's cheeks flushed the tiniest bit whenever she received a compliment. It made him want to take every opportunity to tell her something nice.

After Dad left, and another half hour with the two of them exploring the various systems available out there, they shut down the laptop. It was the closest they'd been since the spread-tasting incident, and he liked every moment.

"Your dad's so nice. I'm leaning toward his suggestion, too." She showed her gratitude with a hug.

"No harm in trying it out," he said, thinking he had a problem with how much he liked her hugging him.

When she released him, she pushed the plate of cookies at him. "Please take these home for your dad."

When her nearby twins heard what she'd said, they both grabbed another treat, nearly emptying the plate. Soon, Mark left without a single moment completely alone with Laurel. But at least he had all the quick and flirty glances they'd shared before, during and after lunch, and while filming the virtual tours, and that great hug to remember.

As it turned out, between her busy schedule and his hotel projects, those not-so-subtle glances were all he had to hold on to for the rest of the week.

The following Friday morning, Laurel couldn't contain her excitement, and fear. Three local travel agents had responded to her outreach and were coming for a trial stay at Prescott B&B. They'd spend a few hours taking a tour and learning the history of the house, exploring the six guest rooms, testing the beds, reviewing her breakfast menu and sampling the wine and appetizers. Then Saturday morning they'd come back for breakfast.

Mark was working on The Drumcliffe gazebo on

the side yard, the project Peter had helped him with last weekend. Being the first person she wanted to share her news with, she took off across the street.

"Mark! You won't believe this."

He grinned the moment he saw her, and after the cat-and-mouse week they'd spent, with her wondering how to move forward after their romp in the ocean and inaugural kiss, that smile made a huge impact. Her grin was because he happened to be working with his shirt off. Yowza!

"Good news?" He got off his knees and stood, making the display of flesh over muscle nearly blinding.

She had to regather her thoughts, and redirect her line of vision. "Oh. Yes, the best!" She explained the plan for the night, which he was crazy about, even hugged her, which really felt great, and a little naughty considering his being shirtless. She'd missed the scent of warm man skin. Once again having to compose herself, she moved forward with her plea. "The thing is, when they get here, I'll need someone to watch the girls while I give the tour and the open house."

"And Peter isn't available?"

"Peter promised to stay in his room and play video games. If he watches the girls, I can't guarantee a problem won't break out, or that the twins might make a racket or yell at him."

He scrunched up half of his face, and not because the sun was in his eyes. "Are you asking me to babysit?"

Put like that, blunt, it did sound horrible, and completely inappropriate. She cleared her throat, knowing the request was unreasonable, but not having a plan B. "Not, uh, in the traditional se-sense," she stammered. "Just maybe sit with them in their room, keep them quiet for like a half hour, forty-five minutes tops, while I give the tour."

He stood there shirtless, staring at her, looking, maybe, incredulous? "You hadn't thought about this part? When you start having guests? What the kids would do?"

Now she felt like a total fool, but the truth was out. Until she had regular B&B guests, and she could afford to hire a babysitter, her best idea was to make them stay in their rooms and be quiet. But four-and-a-half-year-old twins didn't know the meaning of the word. "I'll work this out better in the future, I promise, but is there any chance you can sit with them at four today?"

He shrugged, noncommittally. "Skip Peter's surf lesson?"

"He's okay with that, I already asked him last night."

Mark had seen Laurel in all kinds of sticky situations over the past two weeks, since the day he'd met her, but he'd never seen her looking desperate before. So he gave her outrageous request—thirty-one-year-old man, not the father, babysitting her daughters—a second thought. And agreed. But only because he really liked her. Really liked her.

At quarter to four, he'd showered and changed clothes and strode across the street. When he hit the porch of the B&B, he could hear Claire's and Gracie's squeals and laughter. Good point about keeping them quiet when the guests arrived. But what about during the Saturday morning breakfast for the guests? Who'd watch them then?

He tapped on the door.

"Is he here?" the girls sang aloud in unison.

"Calm down," Laurel instructed, just before she appeared at the door looking fantastic. Wow. She'd put her hair up, and wore a sky-blue patterned sheath dress that showed off her legs, the matching blue pumps helping highlight those shapely calves. This was a sophisticated side he hadn't seen before, and he really liked it. She was nothing like the girls he used to date. Heck, a woman like her would've never given him a second glance. Maybe that was why he was watching her kids instead of taking her out to dinner? Insecurity wasn't appealing and it was time to change. *Step up, Delaney.*

"Hi," she said, stress and worry ruining her overall appearance.

"You look great."

"Thanks." After a quick sigh of relief, she let him in.

The girls jumped up and down, wearing what looked like frilly fairy outfits, one neon pink, one lime green. "We're gonna have a tea party!"

He wanted to address Laurel's nerves, give her a pep talk or something, but he was being swarmed by the little ones. "You are?"

"No, *we* are!" Claire clarified.

Gracie gave an excited giggle, her fingertips in her mouth.

Mark slowly cast his gaze in Laurel's direction. "We are?"

Her brows came together, making a single quote mark above her nose, as she mouthed, *sorry.*

"Whose idea was this?" he addressed the fairies in a tolerant way.

"Mine!"

"Mine!"

Now they were jumping, and in five minutes Laurel's first-ever guests, local travel agents who could make or break her opening, were set to arrive. "Well, as my grandda always says, in for a penny, in for a pound." He clapped his hands. "Let's do this." Then herded them toward their room.

"I owe you," Laurel said quietly when they hit the hall.

"Oh, yes, you do," he replied, rounding the corner.

She closed the doors, shutting off the family quarters from the rest of the house. Though feeling suddenly trapped, Mark opted to concentrate on several great ideas for how Laurel might pay him back.

"Okay, girls, whenever you go to a tea party, you have to talk quietly." He gulped when he saw the tiny table set and ready to go, with three pip-squeak-sized chairs, one obviously meant for him. Managing to get one bun on it, with his knees nearly up to his chin, he worried the chair might break. But so far so good.

The tea was water, but the cookies were fresh-baked snickerdoodles, so it wasn't all bad. And most important, the girls were following his rule and talking quietly. But how long would that last? If he stayed sitting so low to the ground, would they want to style his hair? Put play makeup on him?

After they finished off the cookies in record time, he got a bright idea.

"Hey, you want to watch me hammer some nails?"

"Yes!" they blurted loudly in unison.

"Shh, shh, shh. Remember the tea party rules," he whispered, and they immediately went quiet. "Okay, follow me."

With his index finger covering his mouth, he took them tiptoeing through the kitchen and out the back door, around the side yard, which had been cleaned up immaculately from the first time he'd seen it, and then headed across the street for the gazebo frame, one twin holding on to each of his hands.

Once on the grass, the girls went directly into play mode and started jumping and dancing around. He picked up a hammer, recovering some of his masculine dignity, and while they frolicked, he began some work.

"Can I try?" Claire asked a few short minutes later, pushing her glasses up her nose.

"Me, too?" Gracie.

So he let them both have a turn. Claire aimed for the nail he held in place with puppy-light taps. When Gracie took her turn, she got serious and wound up like a member of a prison chain gang, coming down hard on the nail head, but hitting Mark's index finger and thumb instead. Mostly his thumb.

"Son of a—" He jumped up, shaking off the pain, biting out the words. His lips came together to form a b, but he hesitated as he glanced at his tiny charges, dressed like frilly fairies, eyes wide like elves. *"—building block!"*

Yeah, Laurel definitely owed him.

"And who might these wee ones be?" Grandda appeared out of nowhere.

Mark pretended nothing was wrong with his hand. "Uh, this is Claire and Gracie, Laurel's daughters."

"She give 'em to you, did she?"

"Just for the evening. Can I help you with anything, Grandda?"

"No," he said, while looking as though he had a dozen more questions. "Just thought I'd be pulling a handle for a pint, wondered if you'd care to join me."

Mark glanced around at the girls twirling in circles to make themselves dizzy, giggling all the way. "Thanks for thinking of me, but I can't."

On the periphery, Mark noticed movement and

turned to see Peter crossing the street with a sour expression. Grandda looked even more interested, so he stuck around.

"Come to help out?" Mark said when Peter joined him at the gazebo frame, suspicious of the reason for his visit.

"No." He pouted and didn't make eye contact.

"Looks like you've been sucking a lemon. Lose your video game?"

"No. Mom said I have to watch the girls in the morning, get them out of the house, when the people come back for breakfast."

"So?"

"I'm supposed to meet someone tomorrow morning."

The girls were cute and fun, and generally easygoing, but, as a grown-up, Mark could appreciate the fact they were wearing fairy outfits. With Peter finally reaching out trying to make new friends, Mark could understand how uncomfortable he might feel, when nothing mattered more than what your peers thought of you.

"I get it, but she needs your help until she gets the business off the ground. And I bet, just in case the person you're meeting tomorrow is a girl from your class, she'd think they're adorable. Why not just buy everyone ice cream instead of fighting it? It might work out in your favor."

Peter poked at a rock with his flip-flop-exposed toe rather than answer, but Mark was almost positive he was onto something with the "girl from your class" guess. He could also understand how a guy might want a first meet with a girl to be just the two of them.

"You two look to be about my little Anna's age," Grandda said, ignoring Peter's sour attitude, and grinning at the bubbly twins.

Then it hit Mark. Anna! Of course, why didn't he think of that? He dug his cell phone out of his jeans pocket and dialed Daniel. "Hey, what's Anna doing tomorrow morning?"

"Well, hello to you, too. I'm at work, don't really know. Let me ask Keela."

"Could you ask her if Claire and Gracie can come to play tomorrow morning, say around nine?"

A minute later, while Peter hung close, waiting for his verdict to come in, Keela came on the phone. "That'd be fine. We can take them all to the park for the morning. I've been meaning to have them over for a playdate anyway. May I ask why *you're* askin'?"

Mark looked Peter in the eyes. "Just trying to help out a friend."

He thought he saw a twitch at the corner of the boy's mouth.

Then he realized how that might sound to Keela, who couldn't see Peter. Now he'd probably get grilled by Daniel about Laurel. "Okay, thanks. Gotta go."

And speaking of Laurel, she was crossing the street in that pretty dress with a victorious grin, as three cars drove off behind her.

"Now you're free to help me on the gazebo tomorrow morning," Mark said to Peter, getting the reaction he'd expected…happy about getting out of babysitting, but frustrated he'd been tricked into helping Mark another Saturday.

If Mark wasn't mistaken, Grandda's interest picked up a notch as Laurel got closer.

"So how'd it go?" Mark asked.

"Terrific!" Her smile spoke a thousand words. He liked how that looked.

On reflex, he hugged her—a congratulatory hug—

soon realizing the huge mistake in front of his grand-father. "That's great."

"They gave me so much positive feedback, I'm reel-ing. Now all I have to do is wow them with my famous peach-stuffed French toast tomorrow morning."

A throat cleared. Loudly. Grandda.

"Oh, hey, Grandda, have you met Laurel Prescott yet?"

"Not yet." He reached out his hand to shake. "'Tis a pleasure." Grandda slid a knowing sideways glance at Mark. Daniel and Keela weren't the only ones he was sure to get grilled by.

"Same here," she said. "I hope you don't mind my entire family being camped out in your yard."

"Not at all. The more the merrier, I always say. Right, Marky, my boy?"

Oh, yeah, Mark would have a dozen questions to an-swer the moment he was alone with his grandfather. But right now, Mark didn't care because he was racking up the IOU notes from Laurel. "So I just solved your prob-lem about tomorrow morning. Or maybe I should say, Peter's problem. The girls have been invited to spend the morning with Keela and Anna at the park."

Laurel's eyes widened as she inhaled. "That's fabu-lous. Thanks so much." She shifted her gaze to her son. "Looks like you're off the hook, Peter."

"Not," Peter grumbled.

"He's going to help me raise the roof on the gazebo tomorrow afternoon."

Laurel shook her head, a twinge of disbelief in her eyes. Yeah, Mark could work wonders when he had to. "You are blowing my mind with your thoughtful-ness. I owe you big-time." She hugged him again and squeezed her arms tight around his back, and his bright idea seemed completely worth it. "Thanks so much."

"As a matter of fact, you do owe me. I was thinking tomorrow night Peter could babysit, since he owes me, too, so I can take you to my favorite seafood place up the road." He hadn't actually been there yet, but something told him the restaurant would indeed become one of his favorites, if present company was included.

Surprise tinted her eyes as her smile widened. "That sounds great."

"On one condition."

She tossed him a "there's more?" glance.

First he noticed Peter had been roped into twirling his sisters by holding them under their arms, so he was sufficiently distracted. Then he glanced back at Laurel. "That you wear that dress and your hair up just like that."

Her face relaxed into a lazy grin. "I think that's doable." Her voice sounded lower. Sexier?

And they were flirting, in front of his nosy grandfather, who, if he knew the man at all, was anything but distracted by the kids' playing. He could also feel his grandfather's stare, the heat gathering on the back of his neck. So Mark turned to look at him, seeing that annoying I-believe-in-selkies twinkle in his eyes. And tried to ignore it.

"Well, I'll be off for a pint now. Nice to meet you, Laurel, Peter, Gracie and Claire." He gave a direct look to Mark. "I'll talk to *you* later."

Not if Mark could avoid it!

It wasn't until Laurel gathered up her kids and headed for home that it hit Mark. *What did I just do?* So caught up in the moment of victory for Laurel, he'd forgotten. He wasn't ready to date yet. To have a normal life again. Was he? The thought of socializing with Laurel for an entire evening made his palms sweat because she was out of his league. They didn't have anything in common beyond his helping her fix things, or his looking after her kids. She'd probably said yes only because he'd put her on the spot. Seriously, what did he have to offer a woman like her? She knew what she wanted for her future, and he was still avoiding his. She'd probably be bored out of her mind having dinner with him. Big mistake asking her to dinner, when he wasn't sure he was ready.

Even if he was thinking about dating and getting involved with a woman again, why pick a sophisticated woman with a family to complicate things, and what could he possibly have to offer her in return? Once she got to know him better, she'd discover how humbly he lived at the family hotel, when she'd been married to a man who'd provided for her and three kids. He couldn't possibly measure up. And probably lose interest. Then how awkward it would be to see her across the street every day.

All the good feelings he'd been enjoying, before insecurity snuck in seemed to swirl tight and settle in his gut as he watched the family walk away, little Gracie turning to smile and wave one last time. If she was looking for security, he wasn't her guy. Nor did he want to be.

He bit his lower lip and went back to work, even though his thumb still throbbed. As he hammered a few more nails, he made a snap decision to not think about dinner out tomorrow with Laurel as a date, that way if things didn't work out, he wouldn't feel as bad. He'd call it payback. She owed him for watching the girls and setting up a playdate so Peter could meet that "someone from school" without dragging his little sisters along.

In case his rationalizing wasn't strong enough yet, he'd also look at it this way: it served in his best interest. Asking Laurel to dinner was convenient, because he'd wanted to eat at The Grilled Sea, a new seafood restaurant in Sandpiper Beach, for the longest time. But he hadn't wanted to go there alone.

So their plans for dinner out were all about calling in a return favor.

Not a date, which he still wasn't ready for. Just payback and convenience.

He'd made the mistake of asking a lady or two out when he'd first come home, and quickly discovered he wasn't ready for casual dating or being social yet. Both evenings had been painfully long and squirm-worthy. So putting that different spin on tomorrow night's plans would take the pressure off. Otherwise, he'd be an anxious wreck for the next twenty-four hours over a date with a woman that interested him. He'd spent enough time being anxious when he'd first been discharged and had to deal with PTSD, and he didn't want to go there again. Things had settled down on that level, but being attracted to Laurel, the thought of just the two of them, made him nervous. Which meant she was special.

Stomething about Laurel made him want to give it a shot again.

Saturday night, still reeling from her successful preview Friday evening and Saturday morning, plus the fact she'd received her very first B&B reservation shortly after, Laurel decided to break one small portion of her promise to Mark. She wanted to wear her hair down. The decision was based on jitters and uncooperative fingers. Truth be told, she was more nervous about her dinner date with Mark than the three mock guests yesterday and this morning combined, and she'd been extremely edgy about that. Couldn't do a thing with her updo.

A date? Was that what this was? Or merely "payback" as Mark had insisted. She hadn't been on a date since college, when she'd met Alan. The significance of Mark's being her first date in nearly sixteen years made her eyes water. He was a nice guy on top of being sexy in a clueless kind of way, and she'd been smiling a lot more since he'd shown up to help her unpack two weeks back. What about the finger lick? OMG, what had she been thinking? She'd just wanted him to try her sandwich dressing, and before she knew it, she'd stuck her finger in his mouth. The zing that'd set off zipped up her arm and shot straight to her lady parts. She couldn't deny she had a secret crush on the sexiest handyman she could ever imagine, or that she wanted to look good for him, but what did that mean? Anxiety streaked through her. Letting herself feel again? Her pulse tapped quicker in her chest.

The B&B was finally opening, and she'd be busier than ever. Her children had to come first, the B&B a close second. Anything else would have to come a distant third. She wouldn't have time to get involved with anyone. With him. *Say it, say his name.* Mark. Her pulse settled down a bit.

She stared into the mirror, checking her freshly applied lipstick after saying his name so quietly, she had to read her own lips. This one date couldn't and wouldn't lead to anything else. He said she owed him for watching her kids, which logically meant she should be buying him dinner.

Maybe that's what she'd do, insist on buying their meal. It would send the message their debt was settled and they could revert to business as usual…once she found a babysitter.

Laurel made a mental note to find a trustworthy teenager, preferably a girl who could enjoy Claire and Gracie, no matter what they wore. Then Mark could be kept at a safe distance and go back to being the handyman at The Drumcliffe. He would be a secret crush she could safely keep and explore for those times when she felt completely alone. Which, with a new business and three kids, was bound to be rare.

The doorbell rang. It turned up the dial on the tiny nerves already jumping around in her stomach. Now a full-out gymnastics routine took place, and she could imagine not being able to get a single bite of dinner down.

Suck it up, buttercup. Regardless of how you've rationalized it, you're on a date!

Laurel rushed to open the door, but Peter had beaten her to it. Mark and her son stood at the entrance casually talking about surfing, from what she could hear.

"Hi," she said, sounding far too breathy to be casual. *Gawd!* Her cheeks went warm.

Mark glanced toward her, and she saw that look again, the one he did a terrible job of concealing, where his eyes lit up with interest. She swallowed against her dry throat. Thank goodness Peter was clueless about such looks yet. At least she hoped so.

"Hi. Ready to eat?" Mark sounded bright, unlike her, relaxed.

Ready to eat? No! "Absolutely." *Switch to Mom mode, keep things business as usual.* "Peter, don't let the girls stay up past their bedtime, and they can have one cookie each, but no more sugar before bedtime, okay?"

"Got it, Mom." He gestured for her to leave.

With the tall, good-looking man? What was wrong with her boy?

Mark smiled wide when she stepped onto the porch. He cocked his head toward the curb, and Grandda sitting behind the steering wheel of a four-seater electric golf cart. What?

"He's dropping us off. I figured after dinner we could walk home. It's not far," Mark quickly added before she had the chance to say a peep.

The guy was full of surprises. Even to the point of putting his hand at the small of her back to guide her down the stairs to their awaiting golf cart. It burned through her dress.

Padraig Delaney offered her a toothy smile, just before she and Mark took the back two seats. "At your service."

"This is different," she said.

"One of the perks of living in a sleepy beach community after summer. No one cares!" he said, smiling at her. "No speeding, Grandda." He didn't bother to move his line of vision.

The long, appreciative stare made her antsy.

"Why ruin all my fun?"

She had to admit she enjoyed his Irish accent, but her smile jolted backward along with her neck when the old man put the pedal to the metal and nearly peeled out from the curb.

Mark grabbed her hand and squeezed. Another highly disturbing gesture, though one she appreciated considering she felt she'd just entered Mr. Toad's Wild Ride.

Due to the transportation, they'd taken the back route, alleys and small side streets, so they entered The Grilled Sea through the back door. The restaurant was small but stylish, and they were seated immediately near a window overlooking the ocean. *So he'd made reservations.* He'd done some planning ahead, another good quality.

"I've walked by this place a dozen times," he said, "—even looked at the menu posted out front, but've never eaten here. My mom keeps her ear to the ground in Sandpiper, and she's only heard good things. I hope you like it."

"I thought you said this was your favorite seafood place?"

"After tonight, I'm pretty sure it will be. Anyway, I hope you like it."

"I'm sure I will." *I'm sitting with a guy with amazing eyes, who's shaved and brushed his rich dark hair that curls just beneath his earlobes. A guy who smells good, and who's wearing a heather-gray Henley shirt and jeans that fit just right.* Why wouldn't she like it here?

After they'd both ordered an appetizer and an adult beverage, she broached the subject. "You said I owed you for yesterday, yet here you are inviting me out to dinner. Shouldn't I be paying?"

He stopped midbite of the recently served shrimp cocktail, his brows crunched down. "What sense would that make?"

"The thing is, it doesn't make sense this way. You can't possibly consider me your reward." Okay, she was fishing for a compliment big-time, but she *was* curious. Was this a date, or just payback?

His brows relaxed, a sly smile creased his lips. He was playing along. "Like I said, if I didn't have you to bring here, I still wouldn't know if the food was good. You're doing me a favor."

Definitely playing along.

"You're that averse to eating alone?"

He took a drink of his beer. "I usually have two choices. Either I eat quick and alone at the hotel restaurant, whatever special Rita, our seventy-year-old chef, made too much of, or with the entire family on Sunday nights in the pub. I thought it would be nice to eat in a restaurant of my choice with you. That's all."

He looked sincere, though she'd had to drag it out of him. His confession, both sad and sweet, humbled her. She took a prim sip of her wine, as her lashes fluttered. "Well, thanks, then. I'm glad to be of service." She almost threw in *anytime* but held back. Why come off desperate? And truth was, soon she wouldn't have a weekend to herself. Hopefully, for her business's sake.

Her tentative smile made his eyes brighten. "So then I guess it's a good thing you're still not off the hook," he said, then gave a half-cocked smile.

"What do you mean?"

"You didn't keep your end of the bargain. You still owe me."

What was he getting at?

He gestured with his fingers near his ear, making a long flip, as in hair.

She reached for hers, wondering if she had something in it.

"You were supposed to wear it up."

Her gaze widened with understanding. "It wasn't cooperating tonight."

"Next time, then."

Another date? "Uh, okay, I'll try to remember that."

They switched to routine conversation after that, though that one threw her for sure. One date she could gloss over, but a second? Her stomach coiled at the thought of a third.

Dinner was served, and despite her tension, they both

enjoyed sea bass and some amazing potato dish, along with locally grown vegetables, as the menu proudly suggested. And fresh sourdough bread that was out of this world. Laurel had to admit, the food was great, with good presentation, but the company looked far, far better.

She'd decided this meal qualified as a date, even to the point of being chaperoned to The Grilled Sea by his grandfather, who she gathered was a big influence in Mark's life. She could tell by their interactions they loved each other deeply, and, having missed her two remaining grandparents' funerals during Alan's illness, she envied Mark and Padraig for that.

Though she struggled with opening the door to someone else, while the abiding love for Alan, the tragedy that claimed his life and the pain of losing him was fresh in her mind—wouldn't it always be?—Laurel made a conscious effort to let go. Alan had wanted her to restart her life in some way by using his second life insurance policy. Surely, he'd thought about what that could mean, starting over, while still a young woman. Though they'd never broached the subject, she was sure he wouldn't want her to be alone the rest of her life. Not that this meal out with Mark had anything to do with the rest of her life. Oh, why was she even thinking like this when raw and jagged feelings still ruled her nights? She wouldn't wish that kind of pain on her worst enemy.

Regardless of the confusion swirling around her mind, she calmed enough to enjoy the delicious food, even indulged in a second glass of wine, which helped the nerves tremendously. Mark insisted they share dessert. Nothing like a carbohydrate coma to relax a girl. Then they took the long way home by walking along the beach. By now she'd happily accepted that Mark could call this whatever he wanted, but she'd consider it their first date. It was probably the wine, but she also looked forward to the next. If she kept the right attitude, they could be a "for now" kind of thing. Something that apparently they both needed, in order to move on with their lives. Definitely the second glass of wine talking.

She slipped off her pumps as they entered the sand. "Just so you know, I have no intention of swimming tonight."

He grinned. "Me, either. Wet and sandy jeans are really uncomfortable."

Without giving it a second thought, she put her arm through his, and he made room for her tucked close to his torso. They walked closer to the water, keeping a respectful distance from the damp sand, but still enjoying the crashing of waves and seaweed-scented air.

"I said it earlier, but you really blew me away when you arranged for Claire and Gracie to play with Anna this morning. They were still talking about it when I was getting ready tonight."

"Anna's had a hard summer, breaking her leg and all, and your girls need to make new friends, right?"

"Absolutely. Oh, and Keela said Anna's cast comes off next week."

"Great news."

She glanced at the sea, beyond the noisy waves, fluorescent whitecaps here and there, yet looking so calm. Power greater than she could fathom, with a whole different world existing below the surface. Feeling suddenly miniscule, it helped to be anchored to Mark. The thought jolted her, but she didn't let go of him. And something else, a sudden desire, prompted her to say more.

"You're very thoughtful, Mark."

He pulled in his chin, crushing down his brows, in denial.

"No, really you are. Even though you used me to eat out tonight."

He laughed lightly.

"Your words, not mine." She smiled challengingly.

"Well, maybe my thoughtfulness was a little manipulating."

"I'm glad."

His brows shot up.

Oh, what the hell, she really wanted to kiss him again. "Yeah, and I'd like to thank you."

She stopped walking, turned toward him and reached for his jaw, enjoying the smooth skin beneath her fingertips. His eyes darkened and his lids looked heavy as she moved closer. After quickly wetting her lower lip with the tip of her tongue, she kissed him in a way she hadn't kissed a man—her husband—since before the twins were born.

Mark couldn't believe his good fortune. The first foray into kissing Laurel seemed like child's play compared with this. With their bodies tight in an embrace, and their mouths locked together, exploring and tasting, tempting and teasing, he was hungry for more and didn't let his thoughts get in the way. As great as licking her finger had been, this was a whole helluva lot better.

His hands wandered her back, and he reached below the waist of that sexy blue dress he'd asked her to wear, to feel through the material and knead her hip and bottom, which was firm and sexy like he knew it would be. Her knee edged between his legs, halfway up his inner thigh, as she nipped his lower lip with her teeth.

Hold on! She was as into him as he was to her, which definitely leveled the playing field. It wasn't just about his finding the woman sexy as hell. Regardless of where he lived, she obviously found something about him appealing enough to kiss him like she really meant it, and right here and now wasn't the time to question why.

Liking the long-term ramifications of taking this next step or not, kissing Laurel Prescott like the world was coming to an end was an extremely excellent thing.

Chapter Five

After the hot make-out session on the beach earlier that night, and an equally exciting good-night kiss at her front door, reality blindsided Laurel. She couldn't get involved with anyone yet. She was still getting over losing Alan. Even now a whisper of pain circled her shoulders at the thought of falling for someone again, and how everything good could change in the blink of an eye. No way was she prepared for that, not this soon. Not ever? By the way she felt lying in bed, staring at the ceiling with perspiration lining her upper lip, just from merely considering it, it occurred she might never be ready to open up to someone again. It didn't matter how charming or downright appealing Mark Delaney was. Loss and the pain that followed would never be worth it.

After an ongoing inner conversation between the part of herself that was intrigued by Mark and the other cowering part, afraid to ever open up to such heartache and devastation again, it was Thursday before Laurel asked Mark to help at the B&B. And only then because she had no choice.

"I've lost the power in two of the upstairs guest rooms," she said, showing up at The Drumcliffe workshop and toolshed wringing her hands, panicked over losing the guests she'd booked for that weekend equally as strong as the prospect of looking Mark in the eyes again.

Always glad to see her, he turned off the gas soldering torch and laid the copper pipe down. "Sounds like the fuse box might be overtaxed. Where is it?"

"It's not exactly an emergency. I see you're busy, but as soon as you have a chance?"

"I can do this later." He stepped around the workbench.

He'd been making himself scarce all week, like a coward. What guy in his right mind avoided someone who could twist his socks with a kiss? Evidently, him.

Now here she was, looking great, as usual, even though her pupils were wide with anxiety. It made him think how she might look after making love, and all thoughts after that steamed up his work goggles.

Mark moved the eye protectors up to his forehead, so he could see her better. "Let's go."

When they got to the B&B, she pointed him to the pantry, just off the kitchen, and an antiquated box in great need of updating. "I can replace the couple of blown fuses now, but it will only be a matter of time before it happens again. This thing—" he pointed to the wall box "—is in need of updating."

"Oh, great, another expense. This place is turning into a money pit." Back came the anxious gaze.

He took her by the shoulders. "Calm down. I'm in the hotel business, remember? I know guys who know guys. We'll get this fixed at half the cost."

"You can do that?"

Staring into her eyes, he realized she trusted him, and he felt honored. Another thing that messed with his senses, the fact that he wanted her respect, and respect required him to be more than what he currently was—just a fix-it guy. The most he could do now was impress her by getting a deal on replacing her fuse box. So much less than she deserved—which was an accomplished, financially stable and well-adjusted man, far more fitting—but he powered on with what he knew best.

"My grandfather is a sneaky guy," he said, giving half a smug smile while on the verge of divulging a family secret. "He plays golf, looking like an easy loser, makes bets and wins the game. Takes payback in favors. Just about every businessman in the area owes him something. I'll ask about an electrician, see what we come up with, because electrician is above my handyman grade." Wanting more than anything to continue to impress her, he hated admitting this, but he had to be honest.

She took a deep breath, half of her anxiety seeming to let go. "Okay. Thanks. But what about right now?"

"Like I said, I can replace these burnt-out fuses, no problem, but be careful about turning all the lights on upstairs at once, or using the vacuum in one room with a fan on in another."

Her hand flew to her brow. "I've got guests coming tomorrow! How am I going to handle this? I can't exactly tell them to leave the lights off if they put the TV on. Gah!"

"Let me give Grandda a call."

He made the call, and as predicted his grandfather could call in a favor. In the meantime, with three new fuses in place to keep the house running, for now, he let those previous steamy thoughts take over. He'd been avoiding Laurel for a good reason, because all it took was being in her presence to make him forget how not ready for a relationship he was. Though completely in the present, wanting nothing more than to hold her in his arms again, he got an idea, foolhardy as it was, to take advantage of the moment.

After rushing upstairs to turn off all unnecessary lights, while Mark fixed the fuses, Laurel headed back into the kitchen for a quick drink of water. After, she placed her glass on the counter. The room was completely quiet. Figuring Mark was off getting whatever he needed, she relaxed and wandered toward the pantry to see what he'd been doing. When one step away from the door, a hand reached around the corner and grabbed hers. She squealed as she got pulled into the semidark area. Mark.

"You scared the wits out of me," she said, her heart beating in her ears.

He wore an intent look, a heavy-lidded and sexy gaze. Pulling her near, he put his hands on her waist, bridging the short distance with his face, until their lips met.

She hesitated, knowing it was a mistake to do this, but soon, her arms went over his shoulders and her hands around his neck, holding him close as they kissed the heck out of each other. She could get used to this, which frightened her. A little noise slipped from the back of her throat, which he must have liked, because he pressed his hips closer to hers and kissed deeper. The heady feel of every part of his body along the length of hers made her forget her concerns. Her hands rushed across his muscular deltoids, and around to the back of his hips. She pushed him closer, feeling his obvious reaction to their kisses.

It was dangerous taking their attraction further like this. Yet unable to control herself, she moved over him, letting his solid response send randy love notes straight to her center. Wanting to run with the raw physical draw, she'd put the brakes on emotionally. Go slow, but why not take advantage of their little gift?

Yes, she thought. Yes, yes. Until Mark's cell phone blared "When Irish Eyes Are Smiling." To make matters worse, when Mark answered the obvious tune he'd selected for his grandfather, still wrapped in their tight embrace, Padraig was on FaceTime. Her face was right there along with Mark's, no doubt looking flushed and flustered from the best make-out session she'd had since Saturday night at the beach.

"Any word?" Mark asked, recovering quicker than she had. She zipped out of view of the camera, rather than look at that craggy face and the knowing eyes of Padraig Delaney.

"Ted Wright will be around in an hour. I told him to expect cookies and lemonade."

"Thanks, Grandda."

"Yes, thank you," she said off-camera. "I really appreciate it."

Mark moved the phone to capture her again, and she ducked and pushed his hand away, not wanting the old man to see her kiss-swollen lips.

"You're welcome. Carry on," he said before clicking off.

Laurel looked at Mark, leftover lust lingering in his

gaze. Her breasts were still tight, but the call had de-fused whatever mojo they'd been working on. Still her eyes remained on those beautiful blues, until she did the only thing she could think to release the thick sex-ual tension in the tiny pantry. She broke into a laugh, and Mark joined her.

"Whew," she said, jokingly wiping her brow. "Who knows where we would've wound up if he didn't call."

Mark glanced at the long island counter, and some of her lost heat flared up again. He swallowed. "Sorry," he said. "I just can't seem to keep my hands off you."

"Don't you dare apologize." She kissed him one last time, keeping distance between their bodies. "Appar-ently, I've got some baking to do."

She got down to assembling bowls and cups, flour, sugar, butter, the works, measuring and mixing, and heating the oven. Anything to get her mind off the man driving her crazy in the pantry.

He popped in the new fuses and cleaned up around the box, and a few short minutes later, after checking out the upstairs lights, he kissed her cheek and took off.

Holding a large stainless steel bowl, mixing butter and brown sugar, she stared out the window and let her-self imagine what might have happened if they hadn't gotten that damn, but necessary, call.

Then reality kicked in, flooding her with memories of the pain and loss when Alan died, and she thanked her lucky stars nothing had happened with Mark.

Less than a week later, Wednesday midmorning, Mark, still fixated on memories of an exceptionally hot kiss with Laurel, put the finishing touches on the white-shingled roof of the hexagonal-shaped gazebo.

He'd wanted to leave the cedar wood alone with a natural stain, but his mother had her own plan.

"If we want to use this for weddings, it has to be white," Maureen said, her ginger-colored hair lifting with the light breeze.

"But it looks so classy this way," he said, at the top of the ladder.

"You can leave the floor natural wood with a polyurethane stain, but honestly, honey, our whole point of building this was for weddings. And weddings say white."

"Whatever." He'd learned throughout his life, once his mother got an idea in her head, she couldn't be convinced otherwise. "I'll have Peter help me paint it this weekend."

"Thank you." Maureen stopped momentarily as his words sunk in. "You mean that boy?"

"Yeah, the kid I'm giving surf lessons to. It's like payback."

"Sounds fair enough." She lingered, watching him. He could see the battle going on behind her green stare, the dozens of questions she'd like to ask, but had the good sense not to bring up. "Have you thought more about starting surf lessons for our guests?"

"Aren't I doing enough already?" He hated how he'd sounded like a teenager grumbling about chores, but it seemed every day Mom thought up more ways to get him involved in the running of the hotel, and he didn't want to take on anything else.

"I could have sworn you'd offered, that Sunday night at dinner?"

True, he had. In a moment of weakness, when his parents were throwing out ideas for new perks and activities to entice more guests. His new sister-in-law,

Keela, had signed on to give massages, Dan offered to give some talks on the importance of daily exercise, and even Conor thought he could squeeze in an occasional Saturday morning nature hike for guests. What was Mark supposed to do, just sit there and stuff his mouth with pot roast? So he'd thrown out the idea of beginning surf lessons, never expecting his parents to take him up on it. "Did I?" Okay, so he'd play dumb and hope she'd forget the whole thing out of frustration.

"Yes, you most certainly did." She turned in time to see Laurel approaching. "This conversation isn't over."

"Got it. Okay."

It had been nearly a week since he'd stolen more kisses. Things had been going smoothly between them, and their romance had stepped up the more they hung out together. Like they were feeling each other out, sometimes literally, though neither ready for anything full-blown. He'd decided to take his time and enjoy whatever it was they had going on, and Laurel seemed to have the same idea. She was a mom with three kids, and he was a guy who still resisted responsibility. The likelihood of their getting serious was slim, and so far they hadn't crossed any lines. Though they'd come awfully close that day in the kitchen pantry. For now, that was okay. But he'd been feeling almost happy-go-lucky, something he hadn't felt since high school, and Laurel had everything to do with it.

So he kept telling himself there was no pressure on any level between him and Laurel, just lighthearted flirting and kisses. Mind-boggling kisses. Besides, they wouldn't be able to find the privacy even if they wanted to do more. But he wasn't complaining, he'd enjoy what he had, while it lasted. Some days he even thought he'd found a part of himself he'd lost during the war.

Anyway, she deserved a whole lot more than what little he could offer. In fact, he wondered why she hadn't figured that out already.

"Well, hello there," his mother said. Mark could imagine the raised brow by the tone of her voice.

"Hi, Mrs. Delaney," Laurel said with a smile. "I've come to borrow your son for a quick carpentry issue, if you don't mind."

"Hopefully he has some spare time. I've been keeping him awfully busy."

Could she be more obvious? Something told him he'd be giving surf lessons to more than Peter in the near future, too. Mark climbed down the ladder, his tool belt in place, and approached the women, always happy to see Laurel.

"And please, call me Maureen, we're neighbors."

"Thank you… Maureen."

His mother cast her glance from Laurel to Mark, and he was hit with expectations, hers. The subtle pressure took a little of the shine off his upbeat attitude from seeing Laurel. "Hi. What's up?" he said, enjoying the glint of sun in her caramel eyes.

"I swear this old house shifts overnight. I've got a couple of sticky guest closet doors, and I think they either need to be rehung or have some wood shaved off."

"Sounds easy enough." Since Maureen lingered watching them, Mark kept his distance, but he was quick to decide. "Let's go."

Once inside her house, he followed her up the stairs, enjoying the subtle sway of her jeans-clad hips. At the top, before Laurel had the chance to open the first guest room door, he took her hand and tugged her to him, then dropped a kiss on her lips. It'd been a few days

since they'd kissed, and he didn't feel like waiting another minute.

Her arms circled his neck and she returned the favor
as he walked her against the wall, and leaned in for
more. He nuzzled her neck, enjoying the silky warm
skin and the fact her hair was in a ponytail, clueing
him in this was a workday. Though wanting to linger
right there, kissing and cuddling with the woman who
had his total interest, he understood necking wasn't the
reason she'd come to get him. So after one more thor-
oughly satisfying kiss, one that would leave her crav-
ing more, and him having to adjust himself inside his
jeans, he backed off.

"Is this the room?" he asked.

"Yes," she whispered over his ear, her arms still tight
around his neck.

He edged back, imagining that answer was to a totally different question. Their gazes met and melded
with understanding for an instant, shooting a fine line
of adrenaline down his middle.

"I wish we weren't always in a hurry," she said, a
sincere and inviting glint in her eyes.

"I wish this house didn't have so many bedrooms.
Way too tempting."

That made her smile in a shy way. He touched his
forehead to hers, detecting and enjoying the scent of
fabric softener on her top. On her, even dryer sheet
fragrance was sexy.

"So you gonna let me fix those doors, or are you
gonna keep distracting me?"

She inhaled, a slow smile stretching those delicious
lips. "You started it."

He let his eyes do the smiling, then reluctantly let her
go. Shifting back to business, they went inside where

she showed him the sticky closet door in room number one. He opened and closed it, checked the hinges, ran his hand along the top, then dropped to his knees to check out the bottom.

She'd retreated to the room's exit, but he sensed she still watched him.

"You're the distraction," she said quietly, before leaving the room, and setting the hair on the back of his neck on end.

The house had six fancy guest rooms, but the one room he thought of right then was hers, on the first floor, with the antique bed frame, and the half dozen different ways he'd like to see her on it.

Within a minute of reaching his supply shed to retrieve a scribe tool, a belt sander, a hand-sanding block and sawhorses, his mother reappeared.

"The neighborly thing to do would be to invite Laurel and her family over for dinner Sunday night."

"She's been here nearly a month, and now you're thinking of being neighborly?"

"I took her a welcome basket the week she moved in."

"You did?"

"Yes, I did. We've had several conversations. She never told you?"

He scratched the back of his neck. "Well, it never came up, no."

"Daniel, Keela and Anna are coming Sunday for dinner. This would be the perfect time to have Laurel and the kids over."

Not at all sure if he wanted to share Laurel with his family yet, he hesitated. "Would you like me to invite her?"

Getting the last item he needed, he shut the toolshed. "Nope. I'll take care of it." And he headed back across the street.

An hour later, when the girls were home from school and playing in their bedroom, Laurel sat in the kitchen, sorting through her menu list of special breakfast dishes for the weekend guests. A chorizo, egg, shredded potatoes and cheddar cheese casserole caught her attention.

Mark appeared at the door, and her heart tripped on a beat. Could a man look any sexier than when leaning against a door, arms crossed, in a tight T-shirt and with a tool belt strapped on his low-slung jeans? "All done?" She pretended she hadn't noticed a single sexy thing.

"Yeah, they're both fixed. You want to check before I go?" He hiked his thumb over his shoulder, breaking the picture-perfect pose.

"I'm sure they're fine. Thanks." She put the menus on the island counter and stood. "Can I pay you back with dinner tonight? You, me…and the kids?" She batted her lashes.

"Sounds very romantic." He stepped closer, reaching for her hand. Their fingers played touch-and-go, her daughters giggling and squealing down the hall.

"I know." She sensed the longing in his gaze and wondered if he could read her thoughts. Because lately she'd had plenty. Involving just the two of them. But that would require so many arrangements and preparations, there couldn't be any hope of spontaneity, which used to be most of the fun, as she recalled. A long, long time ago.

"Well, I'm never going to turn down an offer to eat with you, so yes." He caught her hand and laced their fingers together, clamping tight, connecting like a bridge between them. "What time?"

"The usual. After you and Peter get back from surfing. He has a lesson today, right?"

"Yup. Mondays, Wednesdays and Fridays."

Claire and Gracie rushed into the kitchen, running under their arms like a London Bridge is falling down game.

"Okay, then. See you later."

"We're hungry!" In unison.

"One second, girls," she said.

Never breaking from his locked-in gaze, he nodded, letting her hand go, the distance between them growing, then, after rubbing both Claire's and Gracie's mop of hair, under their protest, he started to turn to leave. But two steps in, he swiveled back around. "How about having dinner with my family this Sunday? We always get together in the pub, and Mom makes some pretty spectacular meals. I think Anna's going to be there with Keela and Daniel, too."

"You're inviting my kids, too?"

"Yay," the twins chorused.

"It's a family meal."

She stared at him briefly, touched by the invitation. Getting invited to a family meal was a big deal where she came from, and knowing the Delaney family was close-knit, she also knew his asking meant something. "Then my family and I would love to come."

"Yeah, we'd lovey to go over dere," Gracie piped up.

Laurel smothered a smile, trying to stay on task. "May I bring anything?"

"Nope. Just be prepared for chaos." He looked comfortably resigned to being a part of a big and possibly unruly family, and she envied him for that one instant before he turned and left. "See you later," he called out as he hit the front porch.

"Bye!" loudly from the twins.

See you later. The words sounded so normal. Come to think of it, since moving to Sandpiper Beach, things really had normalized, which was saying something for the long-suffering Prescott family. They'd developed a routine that didn't center on their father's illness. The stress that used to hover over them seemed to have dissipated, and in its place, laughter had returned. Even Peter seemed okay now with the move and starting high school, though she had a hunch a girl at school had a lot to do with it. Bottom line, she was becoming part of a community, making friends, and dare she say it, acquiring a boyfriend?

A warm feeling wrapped around her shoulders. She thought of Mark and his *see you later* promise. The man was sweet and sexy and so damn handy! Buying a B&B without any experience in running it had been the craziest idea she'd ever had, but maybe it was also the best idea she'd had since becoming a widow.

If she kept whatever she and Mark had brewing between them in perspective. It couldn't go anywhere. She was a widow, two years in, but still mourning Alan, struggling to care for and raise her children, and Mark's attention was a boost to her flagging ego. She had four years on him, and a world of pain in her résumé.

Though he'd been in the army, he still lived with his family and had the secure job of helping run an established hotel. The way she saw it, he was worry free with few responsibilities. Yet she sensed something deep and painful ran through him, and she could see it in his often-forlorn eyes.

He'd been away, in the service, in the Middle East. They'd only touched on the topic. Maybe that was the key to why a guy like him preferred to play cat-and-mouse romance with her, rather than a host of women who didn't come saddled with kids and obligations. Younger women who'd jump at the chance if he'd only look up and out instead of down. Or in her case, across the street.

It would be interesting to see how he interacted with his family, and maybe Sunday night, if she got the chance, she'd ask him more about his time in the military.

Sunday night, Mom decided to get everyone involved in preparing the meal. Mark had been assigned grilling duties on the hotel patio for the huge salmon fillets she'd purchased from the fish market at the pier earlier that morning. Off to the side he also grilled a few turkey hot dogs for the twins and Peter, in case they weren't seafood lovers.

One of the best parts of fall by the central coast of California was enjoying the excellent "summer" weather after the tourists had all gone home. Early evening, it was still light and warm, and the coastal water was only a few shades darker than the bright blue sky.

He waved the cedar plank smoke away, still managing to get some in his eyes and blinking hard, then looked up to see Peter and the girls crossing the street. Behind them, materializing through the haze like a lovely dream, came Laurel in a sundress.

He blinked again, then smiled, his body sparking to life. When she waved and grinned, all seemed immediately right with the world. Which worried him. Was he ready for what that meant, stepping up his game to be worthy of her attention...and affection?

"Hey," she said, when they'd reached the patio.

"You look great." He wasted no time spilling his thoughts. "Pretty dress."

"Thanks. I bought it, and a couple others, for the days I greet my guests. Figured I needed to look like a proper hostess." She curtsied and gave a light self-deprecating laugh, as though she could only hope to play the part. He knew otherwise. She was born for hosting a fancy guesthouse.

The white with bright flowers patterned sundress had a wide V-neck with simple cap sleeves, a fitting bodice and a semifull skirt falling just below her knees. Sort of like something from an episode of *Mad Men*. She came off sophisticated and all woman, and so out of his league. Yet here he was, staring too long and wishing they were alone.

"How's the fish comin'?" Grandda appeared out of nowhere, wearing a canary-yellow sweater vest over a goldenrod plaid short-sleeved shirt. How could Mark miss him? The eighty-five-year-old stopped short of the grill and let out a long low whistle. "That dress will get you through all the right doors, it will." He slid a sly and loaded-with-meaning glance Mark's way.

Mark ignored it and went back to watching Laurel.

Laurel blushed and smiled. "Thank you." He waited for another curtsy, but it didn't come. *I guess she only does that for me.* The thought revved him up more, and he counted the moments until he could get some personal time with Laurel.

Daisy, his brother Daniel's Labrador mix—the dog he and his brothers shared duties over when they used to all live in the same hotel suite—broke out of a car that had just pulled up and chased away the lingering moment. Good, too, before things could get awkward with overstated compliments from old men and Mark's ogling eyes. The last thing he wanted to do was make Laurel uncomfortable because he was having a hard time controlling himself.

The blondish dog raced toward Peter and the twins, who squealed with glee and chased her around the yard. A friend to all, Daisy romped on the grass and loved it.

"Danny my boy is here!" Grandda announced, switching his attention from Laurel to the midsized power-red car that had just parked on the street at the base of the long yard.

His brother, who'd let Daisy out, and Keela, his wife, soon followed. From Mark's assessment, Keela didn't look pregnant, though she was at least three or more months, since she was due in April. They exchanged friendly waves with him since he was chained to the grill. He glanced at Laurel, who looked as happy as his grandfather to see them. Last, Anna got out with one huge thing missing.

"Look at me!" Anna crooned. Her cast was gone. The one she'd had to wear since early summer, after falling into a slack at the huge sand dunes down the way and breaking her leg while running with Daisy.

The twins stopped playing with the dog when they saw their new friend, then clapped, seeing her without her full leg cast. "Yay!" they sang and danced around. Anna walked gingerly to meet them, one leg noticeably thinner and whiter than the other. When they met up, they all squealed together.

Daniel climbed the slope of the grass, his hand guiding Keela along, looking happier than he'd been since he was a carefree kid. His physical medicine clinic was becoming a success, and he'd met and married Keela after a horrible breakup with another woman, a woman who'd left him heartbroken and lost, and who'd never loved him back. Then he met Keela. Chalk one up for Grandda and his selkie-lore promises. Whatever caused the change, life was good for Daniel, and it showed.

Mark and Daniel shook hands just as a sheriff's sedan pulled up and parked behind Daniel's car at the curb. Conor soon got out in full uniform, looking all business, but when he saw his brothers, his stern face—a look Mark had gotten used to seeing on his younger brother since returning home—broke into a smile. If you could call that nearly pained expression a smile. He always planned his Sunday dinner breaks around the weekly family-meal hour.

"Everything's ready on this end," Mother called from the pub's side door. "How's that salmon coming?"

Mark waved away more cedar plank smoke. "We're good to go," he said, transferring the fish to the huge platter his mother handed him. She noticed Conor and Daniel and Keela and Anna without her cast, and Laurel with the twins and Peter, and left Mark holding the plate, salmon and all. She hugged and greeted each one, her face radiating joy so deep Mark couldn't help but grin along.

A sharp whistle from the same pub door ripped the air. His father Sean stood in the same doorway Maureen had just exited, his head nearly touching the top. "Dinner's ready. Let's go!" he called out, benevolently herding his family inside, then greeting everyone as they passed with a fatherly hug and a deep-hearted smile.

Mark hung back, waiting for Laurel and her kids, escorting them inside.

Sean grinned at Laurel.

"I signed up for that free trial," she said on her way in.

"Great!" He squeezed her arm like they were old friends. After a quick nod, Peter, in usual form, slipped past, when Sean squatted to greet the little girls. It would be their first experience with "dinner" at the family pub. *Oh, boy!*

"I hope you're ready for this," he said to Laurel, knowing there was no way a person could prepare for it.

Her soft hazel-brown eyes crinkled, glistening with the golden autumn sun and happy vibes.

Ready or not, it was time to break bread with the Delaney clan.

After a typical unruly dinner, life still managed to feel good, sweet and filled with possibilities, which put Mark on edge. Until he put his arm around Laurel, who'd managed to stay bubbly throughout the meal, answering questions flying from every corner of the table. Her confident, positive and humble attitude was a huge draw for Mark. And though preferring to be the strong silent kind of guy, she had a way of helping him open up.

He'd laughed along with just about everyone else at Grandda's silly jokes, made eye contact with every person when they spoke, and he'd snuck as many glances at his good-looking date—if that's what he should call it—as possible without getting caught.

He had been caught, though, and not just by Grandda with his knowing stare, or his mother, who returned some sort of hopeful gaze, but Peter, too. The kid had been especially quiet during the meal, and seemed to keep his eye on his mother. Mark wasn't sure how a boy still mourning his father might feel about his mother getting attention from another man. He suspected not good, but it was too late to turn back now. Mark Delaney had a thing for Laurel Prescott, and feeling more

like his old self than he had in a long time, he thought
he might give whatever they had going on a chance.

Hopefully Peter would understand.

He would also make a point to bring up the subject
of *Laurel + Mark* tomorrow afternoon when he gave
Peter his surf lesson. Maybe ask Peter for permission
to date his mother. He'd planned to butter him up with
a surprise—his own board, an old one Mark had been
refurbishing in his spare time. He'd removed the wax,
fixed the dings, even put on a new, thicker traction pad,
and couldn't wait to see Peter's reaction. From the glum
expression he'd worn throughout dinner, Peter could
use a happy surprise.

The best part about the family pub dinner on Sunday
nights was that the hotel restaurant waitstaff cleared
the table and cleaned up. After the meal, as everyone
meandered toward the family-styled chair groupings in
another corner of the pub, he saw Grandda single out
Laurel. Not a good thing. But Conor had to get back to
work, and he wanted to talk to Mark.

"I was thinking of going to check out the Beacham
house tomorrow, and wondered if you wanted to come
along."

The Beacham was an old, run-down Gothic-looking
house on the cliffs that hadn't been lived in for over a
decade. Conor was fixated on it, had wanted to buy and
fix it up since he was in high school and dating Shelby.
Why? Mark didn't have a clue. But it was the reason
a man making a perfectly good salary still lived at his
parents' hotel, and life didn't always make sense.

"I've got a surf lesson with Peter at four tomorrow,
but after that, I'm good. As long as daylight holds."

"That's what police tactical flashlights are for."
Conor nearly cracked a smile. "Talk tomorrow, then."

Off he went, stopping long enough to kiss his mother goodbye and shake his father's and Daniel's hands.

He broke up whatever conversation Grandda was having with Laurel—thank goodness—to give the old man a hug, said goodbye to her, then left.

Mark figured now was as good a time as any to rescue Laurel from the farfetched stories Padraig Delaney was known to tell. He stepped in front of Laurel, reached out his hand and, when Laurel offered hers, entwined his fingers through hers. "If you don't mind, Grandda, I don't want to waste a perfectly beautiful sunset." How could Padraig argue? Then Mark guided her toward the outside pub deck.

Just before they hit the door, he caught Peter with a solemn gaze watching them. Yeah, he'd definitely have a talk with Peter tomorrow afternoon. Because the way things were going with Laurel, he wanted to give the kid fair warning.

A few minutes later, Mark and Laurel stood in a secluded corner facing the ocean, forearms leaning on the wooden deck rails, talking.

"Your grandfather told me an interesting story about you and your brothers."

Oh, no, he didn't! Couldn't the man keep his fanciful thoughts to himself just once? "Really?" He tried to sound nonchalant, even though he had a good idea of which "interesting" story Grandda had told her.

"Uh-huh. About a certain fishing trip the three of you took, and a pod of orca…"

"Oh, let me guess, the one about saving the seal who could turn into a selkie and that now owes each of us a favor?"

"How'd you know?" she teased, a playful glint in her eyes.

"You know he's from Ireland, right?"

She laughed quietly. "So, I guess it's true, then?"

"Touché." Mark sighed. He loved his grandfather with all his heart, but once the old man got a notion into his head, he simply couldn't let it go. Having succeeded in predicting Daniel's finding his wife, all because they'd saved a "selkie," he'd moved on to Mark—the middle brother—and his ideas were nothing short of laughable.

Except here he was with Laurel, a woman he'd met a short month ago, feeling things he hadn't felt since before enlisting in the army...

"What exactly is a selkie?"

"They're folklore characters. Seals at sea who shed their skin to become human on land. That's all Grandda's selkie story has in common with the usual myths, where they marry then return to the sea. He insists the seal we saved will return the favor of saving its life by finding each of us a mate. As I said, that's all his embellishment."

"That's kind of sweet, isn't it? Wanting you all to be happy and in love?"

"Sure he'd like to see us all get married, too, but Conor and I both remind him, in our own time. I think because he's halfway through eighty and getting closer to ninety, he wants to rush us."

"Well, I still think that's sweet, and you're very fortunate to have such a great family."

"They were all on good behavior tonight, except Grandda, of course," he teased.

She tossed a look, not having any of it. "Well, it must be nice to have such a support system."

Which made him wonder. "Isn't your family?"

"Yes, my parents were very supportive during Alan's

trials, but I'm an only child. There were many things I would've liked to talk to a sister about." She went silent for a few moments, staring out to sea. "There was only so much I could dump on my friends, you know?"

He put his arm around her shoulders and tugged her near. "I can't imagine what you must've gone through."

"Nor I you." Her eyes found his and held his gaze. Was she referring to his time in the Middle East, and the PTSD he'd had to deal with since being home? He'd only hinted at it over their dinner out. Had Grandda spilled the beans on that one, too? Or maybe Peter had confided in her about some of their conversations in the ocean during surf lessons. "If you ever feel like talking…"

She'd quickly turned the topic back to him. But it'd been a good afternoon and evening, regardless of Grandda's silly ocean tales, and the last thing he wanted to do was ruin it by bringing up old problems. And lately, the same troubles that'd been plaguing him since the end of his military career seemed to be just that— old concerns. Why dredge them back up now, when the sun was setting bright orange and red on the water? With a beautiful woman by his side.

"Thanks, but right now I'd rather do this." He put another arm around her and pulled her flush to his chest so he could let her know how good she made him feel, with a kiss. A kiss that quickly heated up to equal participation and, from the way her hands dug into his back, equal longing. They took their time exploring, enjoying, fanning the coals that always smoldered between them.

"Hey, Mom, I'm going—" Peter stopped short.

They quickly broke off the kiss and turned toward his voice.

He looked confused, maybe a little upset, but covered it up, like he hadn't seen a thing. "—going home now." His voice sounded different on the last phrase.

"Did you thank Mr. and Mrs. Delaney?" Laurel tried to act like she hadn't just been caught by her son making out with a man. A man who wasn't Peter's father.

"Yeah." The teen did his best to act normal. Sullen. "I've got some homework to do." He averted his eyes.

"Where are your sisters?"

"They're playing with Anna and the dog." He wouldn't look at his mother, just stared at the wood planks on the deck.

"Okay. I'll be home soon."

Mark could tell Laurel, though soundly shook up, tried her best to keep it together. But things had just gone wonky, and he sensed payback would be involved. Making Mark wish he'd broached the subject on his mind—dating Laurel, which, after witnessing their kiss, had to officially and obviously be on Peter's mind, as well—yesterday when he'd taught Peter how to paint the gazebo.

Tossing a cold bucket of water on them couldn't have done a more thorough job of putting out the passion they'd been working up.

"I need to talk to him," she said.

Mark saw the near panic in her eyes as she took off after her son.

"I'll have Keela bring the girls over when they go home."

"Thanks," she said, already down the deck stairs and heading for her house.

Confused and worried, Peter rushed blindly across the street for home, to his room, where he slammed the door. Didn't Mom care about Dad anymore? Would he lose her, too, if she fell in love with Mark?

Anger washed from his head downward, concentrating around his chest. It felt tight and hurt. He'd thought Mark was his friend, but now he wondered if they'd been hanging out together only so Mark could get to his mother.

He wasn't a friend. He was his enemy. No way could he talk to his mother about it, because she'd take Mark's side.

There was a knock at his door. "Leave me alone!"

"I want to talk to you," his mother said.

"I said leave me alone!" He hated that his voice cracked on *alone*. He'd locked his door, knowing she'd want to face him after her betrayal.

But there was only one person he wanted to talk to. His dad. And he was gone.

Chapter Six

Monday, Mark waited for Peter at the regular spot on the beach at four o'clock, but he didn't show. He'd opted not to bring the refurbished surfboard, thinking it might come off as a bribe, and now he was glad he hadn't. After Peter's obvious disapproval of the kiss Sunday night, the last thing Mark wanted to do was make the kid angrier.

He waited a full twenty minutes before texting Peter. Where are you?

Nothing. Yeah, the kid was ticked off all right.

After a half hour of riding waves, Mark headed back to the beach and on to the B&B, ready to face Peter and apologize for any distress he may have caused him. But then what? Quit seeing Laurel? Not gonna happen. He'd just found her, and she'd been a great surprise. Truth was, he didn't want to give her up because her son didn't want his mother to have a life after Dad. Peter needed to understand that, ready or not, life kept moving forward. And his dating Laurel didn't mean anything serious would happen. How could it when he hadn't gotten that far in his personal plans? Their dating also didn't mean Peter's life as he knew it would change.

He arrived at Laurel's as she carried two handled tote bags of groceries from the car.

"Let me help you with that," he said, her smile brightening his mood as he took the next two totes out of the trunk, but it always did. Once inside the kitchen, he placed the bags on the island counter. "Is Peter home?"

"Wasn't he supposed to be with you?"

"He didn't show up for his surf lesson, and didn't respond to my texts."

She stopped unloading canned goods and stared at Mark, obviously stunned. In the next second she dug through her shoulder bag for her cell phone and made a call. "Peter, pick up, it's Mom," she said after a few seconds. "Please pick up?" She huffed, the color beginning to drain from her cheeks, and dialed again. His stomach constricted. She dropped her head back in frustration. "It went right to his messages."

Mark stepped forward, touching her unsteady hand. "At least we know he got your call. When's the last time you saw him?"

"This morning." Her eyes glistened with early tears. "He was angry, wouldn't talk to me last night, but he got up and dressed for school like he always does. Didn't say two words to me at breakfast, though." She sniffed and reached for a tissue on the sink counter. "I dropped him off at school before I took the girls to kindergarten. He barely acknowledged me when he got out, just made a grunt when I said I loved him." Her lower lip quivered. "What if he's run away?"

Mark took her into his arms, but she stiffened instead of relaxed. "Don't jump to conclusions. Maybe he's hanging out with his friends and wants to upset us. He'll probably show up for dinner."

Her brows crashed down with a disapproving expression. "I can't wait that long! I need to know where he is now."

"Listen, today's my brother's day off. He can help us."

Panic widened her eyes. "What if he's run away? Where would he go?"

"If he's run off, Conor and I will find him, I promise."

There was only so far a kid could go on foot. Who knew if he had money for the bus. Would he have the nerve or the wherewithal to head back to Paso Robles on his own? Did he know how to get there, and once he got there, what would he do? He'd never mentioned friends back there.

"What's he wearing today?"

She thought for a second, her eyes brightening. "His father's old T-shirt."

"The Bart Simpson one?"

She nodded.

It was probably a clue that Peter had his dad on his mind after seeing his mother with Mark last night. "Where's your husband buried?"

"He's not. He wanted to be cremated, and we scattered his ashes here in the ocean."

He and Peter had talked about a lot of things while they waited for waves. One of them was the best places to have a complete view of Sandpiper Beach and the ocean. "I'm going to check the pier. I'll call Conor and let him know what's going on." He took off running north to the small fishermen's pier.

Mark had told Peter where his favorite spot was when he needed to think. If his father was buried at sea, it might make sense to want to spend some time thinking about him up there.

He got to the pier and asked around, but none of the regular fishermen had seen him. Then he got an idea, a wild idea, but he didn't have a clue where to start. He also called Conor.

"Got a problem. Peter's gone missing. Can you help?"

Within five minutes, Conor met Mark back at the B&B, where he pulled to the curb in his muscle car and waited for Mark to get in. "I called it in. Does Laurel have a recent picture?"

Mark rushed back to the porch. "We need a picture for the sheriff's station."

"No luck at the pier?"

Mark shook his head.

She rushed inside, then shortly back out to the porch. "Just got his school picture last week." She handed a typically uncomplimentary five-by-seven school photo of Peter to Mark, who rushed it back to the car.

Mark dipped his head to Laurel, who waited anxiously on the porch. "Call me the instant you hear from him."

She nodded, obviously trying to keep it together, while having to hang back with her daughters and pretend everything was okay, so they wouldn't freak out, too.

"I'll take this to the sheriff's station," Conor said. "I'll tell them to get all the details from Laurel,"

"Sounds good. I'll check the beach where the school kids hang out," Mark said, taking some comfort in knowing the department didn't waste time on protocol before considering any kid missing. These days, the sooner they were found, the better the chances no one got hurt, whether the kid took off intentionally or not.

Mark figured it only made sense to check the closest locations before heading up the hillside, so he agreed. "Let's go, then. Meet you back here in fifteen minutes."

Conor drove at breakneck speed up the street, and Mark jogged toward the beach and the area where most of the high school kids congregated. As expected, there was a large group of kids, and Mark spotted the group who'd messed with Peter the first day Mark had met him. He approached the tall guy.

"Have you seen Peter lately? He didn't show up for his surf lesson."

The tall kid curled out his lower lip, thinking, then shook his head. "Not here. Saw him in gym class, though."

"What period was that?"

"Fourth."

Before lunch. That could mean anything. "Any of you guys have classes with Peter Prescott?"

"You mean pee-pee?" one smartass replied with a snicker. "Yeah, I've got art with him."

"What period?" Mark ignored the desire to deck the kid.

"Fifth."

"Was he there?"

"Yeah. He's good at painting. Never misses."

He'd figured out Peter's whereabouts up until two-ish. It was nearly five now, and with the days getting shorter, the sun set between six and six thirty, so he rushed back to the B&B and met up with Conor.

"Let's drive by the school," Conor suggested. "Maybe he's still there."

He gunned the engine, and they made it to the high school in near record time. A few stragglers were still hanging around the red brick administration building. Sandpiper High had less than five hundred students, tiny as far as high schools went, which was to their advantage.

"Any of you know Peter Prescott?" Mark asked.

They looked at each other, and one scrawny girl with long brown hair raised her hand.

"You see him after school?"

"Yeah. He was walkin' toward the beach."

Minimal help, but at least he hadn't headed for the city bus system, and they knew his whereabouts until 3:00 p.m. And Mark hadn't seen a hint of him at the pier or hanging out with the other kids on the beach.

"I'm going to follow my hunch on this," Mark said to Conor. "Let's go to the dunes and catch that trailhead."

"The place we used to go?"

"Yeah, the cliffs. Peter and I talked about that place once. Maybe he's hiding out there. He was wearing his dad's old T-shirt today. They scattered his ashes at sea off the pier, but he wasn't there. The ocean's all he's got left of his dad."

"And the view's awesome from there," Conor added.

"Exactly."

Once they parked and took off toward the sand dunes to find the trail up to the secluded cliffs, Mark explained how Peter had caught him kissing Laurel after dinner last night.

Conor tightened his chin with understanding. "That could be tough. How long's his dad been dead?"

"Around two years, I think."

Conor gave Mark a thoughtful glance. "So you and Laurel?"

"Yeah. I think." Mark kept hiking, gravel sliding under his shoes, feeling odd admitting it to his brother. "Probably not after this, though."

"You can't let a kid keep you from seeing her if there's something going on." For being the fittest man Mark knew, Conor sounded very out of breath as they climbed the steepening trail.

"Laurel would be the one to make that decision." Mark used a boulder to propel himself forward. "And honestly, I'm not sure where it's going with Laurel, just that I like being around her, and I'd like to keep seeing her. Beyond that?"

"Well, that's a start, man."

After today, whatever they had going on was probably finished, anyway.

They'd forgotten how tough the hike to the top of the cliffs were. Conor wondered aloud if Peter was in good enough shape to make it.

"He's skinny, but he's been doing the exercises I said he had to, to learn how to surf, and his leg strength has changed noticeably."

"He's got a hundred less pounds to carry up this hill, too." Conor stopped to catch his breath, then used an ancient bush limb to push off again. "At least we got a good workout today."

Mark hoped all their effort wasn't for naught. "We've got to find him. Laurel will freak out if we don't."

"We'll find him."

"Peter!" Mark yelled as they got close to the top of the cliff trail. Nothing.

"Peter!" Conor called out. "If you're there, answer us, man." Nothing.

Then, "Leave me alone."

Mark glanced at his brother and smiled. "Not gonna happen." They reached the summit, and saw Peter ignoring the wood bench, sitting on a boulder instead, knees up, chin resting on top, looking out to sea. He had to be cold with the kicking-up breeze whipping through that oversize, threadbare T-shirt.

"There you are," Conor said.

Mark didn't say another word, just climbed up next to him on the rock and sat, leaving a safe distance between them. Peter glanced at him, anger flashing in his eyes.

"Like I told you that day, I used to come up here to think." He glanced at his watch: ten to six. The sun would set shortly, and if Peter was cold now, he'd be freezing by then. "I hope you got all your thinking done because we need to climb down before it gets too dark to see."

Conor was already using his cell phone. "Laurel, we found him."

"Your mother's been worried sick," Mark said, doing his best not to sound accusatory. "And you must be hungry. Let's get you home in time for dinner. We can talk later."

The boy didn't budge. Mark heard Conor calling the sheriff's station. He reached for Peter's arm, to help him down, but Peter yanked it away. "Look, I get it, you're pissed that I kissed your mom. We can talk about that, but not here. Let's go."

In true Peter fashion, he continued to stare out to sea, doing a great job of pretending Mark didn't exist.

Mark needed to get real. "It's two to one, man. You gonna go down on your own, or are we gonna carry you? Your choice. Either way, we're taking you home. Now."

With his lower lip curled inward, teeth clamped on top, Peter reluctantly stood. Mark offered his hand again. When Peter took it, his eyes had already welled up with tears. Once they were off the boulder and back on the trail, Mark wanted to hug the kid, which surprised him, but he only patted him on the back, not wanting to push his luck. "We'll talk about this all you want. I promise. But first, let's get you home."

Laurel rushed to the car when Mark brought Peter home. She couldn't help the tears of relief, and didn't care if Peter minded if she hugged him. The twins didn't really understand what was going on, but they knew their brother hadn't come home when he was supposed to. She'd made sure they understood he was in trouble because of it. May as well lay down the rules with them now rather than later, when it might be too late. Like today. She'd never expected Peter to run away.

"Where were you?" Claire asked.

"Are you in trouble?" Gracie also asked.

He didn't answer, ignoring them. Surprisingly, Peter let Laurel hold on to him longer than she expected. Maybe he was shook up, too.

"Please don't ever do that again."

His glance shot downward. There was so much to talk about.

Laurel lifted her line of vision and seized the opportunity. "Conor, could I ask you a big favor?"

"Sure."

"Could you watch the twins while we have a talk?"

"I don't want to talk," Peter groaned.

"Too bad, buddy, we're talking. Now."

Conor went still. Quickly realizing he'd been caught off guard, he shifted his eyes to the little ones. She'd left him no choice, and being a conscientious peace officer, she knew she had him over a barrel. "Uh, I guess so."

"Thanks, man," Mark said standing nearby, obviously relieved.

Claire and Gracie looked up toward the sky to be able to take in all of Conor Delaney. They probably thought he was half giant. They'd met him Sunday night, so he wasn't a total stranger, but Laurel sensed their apprehension, since they hadn't interacted much then. She touched both of their shoulders and bent forward. "Conor is Mark's brother. He's a nice man, and he'll watch you guys for a little bit, okay?"

"Okay," Claire, the leader, said.

"Do you play Legos?" Gracie, the practical, asked.

"Sometimes." No longer resisting the last-minute plan, Conor gave a halfhearted smile and followed them inside.

Laurel guided Peter through the door, aware that Mark followed. "Um, Mark, can you make Peter a sandwich? I'd like to talk to him alone for a minute."

"Sure," Mark said.

"Not hungry," Peter mumbled.

"I'm sure you are." Laurel used her eyes to encourage Mark to step out for a little while. He caught on and followed her lead. "Let's go in here." She led the way to the front sitting room, then closed the pocket doors behind her. Peter reluctantly sat, and she sat beside him.

Instead of starting off scolding him for scaring her to death, as she may have earlier, she held back on her emotions and went for the heart of the matter. "First off—" no point in wasting time "—you've got to know that no one will ever replace your father." She took his chin in her fingers and turned his head so his eyes met hers. "He is your one and only father. I wish you'd had

more time with him. God knows, I wish he'd never gotten cancer, but we don't always get our wishes."

Peter must have still been raw from running away
and getting caught by the very person he most likely
never wanted to see again—the man who'd dared to
kiss his mother—because he broke down and cried.

She edged closer to her son and drew him near. "I
know you miss him. I do, too. I know it makes you
angry that he died. It makes me angry, too."

After a few moments of letting Peter get his feelings
out through tears, then offering him a tissue or two,
she continued. "It's been two years since Daddy died,
Peter. I'm not saying you have to forget him. I'd never
do that. We'll both always remember him. But I want
you to try to understand that our moving to Sandpiper
Beach was to help us all move on." She glanced at him
while he blew his nose.

"He's my dad and I'm never going to stop loving
him."

"I'll always love him, too."

"Then why are you kissing *him* and going on dates?"
Peter protested, pulling away from her hug. She could
read his scowl—betrayal. She was a betrayer as far as
her son was concerned. She couldn't let him think that
because the idea broke her already-broken heart.

"Going on a date isn't the same as what Daddy and
I had. But I need friends, too, Peter, just like you do."

"He was supposed to be my friend. Now it feels like
he was only nice to me to get to you."

"I don't believe that. You and I met Mark on the same
day, and since then we've both gotten to know him better. Wouldn't you agree he's a nice man?"

Reluctantly, Peter nodded, obviously hating where
the conversation was going.

"If I like Mark, it doesn't mean he can't be your friend, too."

Peter's angry stare and extra-long sigh made her want to reinforce her original point, because she had a hunch her boy was worried about where he stood in their changing world.

"No one will ever replace your father, or *you*, in here." She pointed to her chest. "We're family. You're my son. I love you more than you can understand."

Things went quiet for a few seconds as Laurel hoped Peter was taking in her declarations. A light tap on the door drew her attention.

Mark opened the pocket doors with a sandwich on a plate in the other hand and a can of soda under his arm. "Okay if I join you guys?"

Peter shot Mark a look that stated he wasn't ready to forgive him for kissing his mother just yet, that maybe he never would. Mark seemed to sense now wasn't such a good time to join in and put the sandwich on the table, then prepared to leave.

"Peter's upset about our dating." Laurel figured Mark deserved an explanation, especially after all he'd done that afternoon and evening searching for her son and bringing him home.

"Peter, I value our friendship—" unfazed by Peter's glower, Mark went on "—and want to keep hanging out, just the two of us. But I like your mother, too. Would it be okay if she and I went out once in a while?"

More silence from Peter, who was definitely not on board with Mom branching out.

"I know you've been through a lot of changes lately, and I thank you for sharing a lot of them with me when we surf," Mark continued. "I don't want to push you, so I'll leave you with your mom for now and we can talk later."

Mark turned to leave. When he got to the doors, he swung around. "I'm glad you're home and safe, Peter. It scares me when my friends go missing." He opened the door.

"Mark?" she said.

He looked back watching Laurel cuddling her skinny son.

"Thank you."

How could he not see the deepest appreciation Laurel could possibly show from far across the room. She'd willed it into him. How grateful she was to him for bringing her son home. Things could have ended up a dozen different ways with Peter's taking off on his own without telling anyone, they both knew it. Surely, his sheriff brother understood.

He nodded solemnly and closed the doors. She offered the turkey and cheese sandwich to Peter and surprisingly, he took half and ate a bite.

"I just want things to be the way they've been, just you and me and the twins," Peter said, his mouth full.

Laurel couldn't let that comment go without a challenge. "Don't I have a say in it? And who says our family unit is going to change just because I go on a date?"

Peter hung his head, looking as though the entire world had just crashed on his shoulders.

"I get that you may feel abandoned by Dad's dying," she said, "Sometimes, I do, too. But get it in your head, I'm not leaving you. You'll be begging me to leave you alone long before I will." She figured a little humor injected into the tension in the room couldn't hurt.

Peter relaxed a tiny bit in Laurel's arms, giving her hope some of the words were sinking in. "You know beyond anything in the world that you're my son and I love you with all my heart."

Peter inhaled a long, ragged breath, and Laurel put her chin on the crown of his head. He'd always be her little boy, even though he was almost as tall as her now. She figured after all he'd been through today, he might want to hear her say it one more time. "I'll never abandon you for anyone else. Please don't ever take off again without telling me where you're going."

"Okay," Peter mumbled, because his mouth was full with another bite of sandwich.

Mark was grateful the kid had made the right choice and come home with him and Conor. He also understood how deeply thankful Laurel was to have her boy home, and that Mark and Conor had brought him. Her sincere thanks was the only payment he needed.

The intense moments had made him thirsty, so he walked to the kitchen to get a drink of water before he left. He heard the girls laughing and making a racket. Then he remembered his brother had pulled bambino duty. The thought made him smile. He tiptoed down the hall to peek a look at how Conor was handling things, but with no intention of taking over. His little brother, who was two inches taller than him, sat cross-legged on the floor, with the twins messily building from mounds of primary-colored click-together blocks.

Seeing his huge brother in that position cracked a smile on his previously grave expression.

He padded back to the kitchen and drank the water. Man, being a parent had to be the toughest job in the world. It was certainly not a job he felt ready for, either firsthand or in a step-in role. He genuinely liked Peter, it was true they were friends, but having the responsibility of being a father figure was a whole different ball game.

Mark had heard enough of Laurel's heartfelt pleas to her son to realize what a great mom she was. How she was nothing like any lady he'd ever been involved with before. And though he was nowhere near ready for anything more than stolen kisses and promising glances, it hit him what a good woman she was. His relationship with Laurel and her kids wasn't for play. It was real, and he better be sure he was ready for it.

That from a guy who didn't even feel ready to take on surfing lessons for guests at the hotel. And he loved surfing!

"Flush, wash and be on your way!" Claire said as the bathroom door closed. Was that for Conor or Gracie?

He gulped down the rest of the water, needing to get out of there but not wanting to get caught by Conor before he left. So he waited until he heard the toilet flush, the water run and the door open and close again. He peeked around the corner again and saw the back of his brother heading into the twins' room. So Claire even bossed big guys around. It made him chuckle inside.

Feeling guilty, he headed down the hall to let Conor know before he left that he was sticking him with the childcare. But he overheard something else first, something he'd never expected to hear in his life.

When we play and make a mess, it's always good to try our best,
To cleeeaaan up.

Conor had taken an old TV jingle and put new words

to it to get the girls to help him clean up the toys. Would wonders never cease? Mark shook his head and smiled, then deciding not to interrupt the little play party, he left for the hotel, because he had a whole lot of thinking to do.

Around eleven, Laurel texted Mark. Feel like talking?

In her usual easygoing way, she'd coaxed him to tell her what was on his mind. *A whole helluva lot!*

After getting chewed out by Conor for abandoning him with the twins, Mark had been sitting on the pub deck thinking thoughts he hadn't expected to think for years yet. About how he might be falling for someone for the first time in…a decade?

He couldn't ignore Laurel's invitation to talk, not after all she'd been through that day. Instead of answering her text, he walked across the street and tapped on her door. When she opened it, it was obvious she'd taken a shower and her hair was still damp. Dressed in pale gray girlie-styled sweats and big fuzzy slippers, she smiled demurely, not saying a word, like she'd been expecting him. As if they belonged together.

When he stepped inside, she hugged him, and he immediately remembered why he'd been thinking about Laurel the way he'd been for the last few hours. She felt right when he held her. Made him want to be around her…all the time.

"You okay?" he asked.

"I needed a hug."

So he hugged her tighter and threw in a neck kiss. "Everyone in bed?"

She nodded. "Want some herbal tea? I just made a pot."

It wasn't his thing, and he didn't want to let go of her, but why not. "Sure."

They strolled to the kitchen, his arm around her shoulders, her arm tucked tight around his waist. She wasn't kidding about having a pot of tea ready. She peeled away from his side and found a small tray, soon putting two of her beautiful bone china English teacups on it, then cream and sugar, and four homemade peanut butter cookies.

"I have an idea," she whispered. "To keep from waking up the kids, I thought we could have tea upstairs."

"Let me carry that for you." He took the tray and let her lead the way to the far end of the second floor. The exact opposite of where her children slept below, he noted. She opened the door to the second-biggest guest room, not the honeymoon suite, but one with ample sitting space, and a gas fireplace that had conveniently already been lit, making the room feel extra cozy. Not to mention the huge bed in the large arched recess. Hmm, she must have been doing some thinking, too?

He set the tray on the coffee table in front of the daintily flower upholstered love seat, then sat.

She stood a couple of feet away, an appreciative look in her eyes. "I owe you a big thank-you for finding my kid."

"Hey, I was glad we found him. All I did was put a few things together and get an idea."

She poured them both some tea, handed him his cup, then sat beside him. "I don't know what I would have done without you today."

He didn't know what he would've done if he hadn't found Peter. "Did he open up more after I left?"

"He told me he trusted you, and got upset when he thought you had used him."

"Damn, that makes me feel horrible."

"I straightened him out. Plus, he believed what you

told him." She took a sip of chamomile tea and stared at him over the cup. "He admits you're a great guy, and I told him that's how I felt, too."

She stopped talking in an obvious *it's your turn* sort of way. He remembered the text and why he'd come over in the first place. "Well, while we're admitting things, I guess I should say, first off, I really do like your son. In fact, I like all of your kids. You've done a great job."

"Thank you. Some days, like today, I'm not so sure."

"Nah, you're a good mother. I can't imagine all you've been through since your girls were born."

Her gaze shifted downward, studying her tea. He could only imagine how hard she'd had it for so many years, and it made those protective feelings he'd been trying to avoid swell up again. "I have to also admit that I, too, really like you." Could he sound stiffer? That was not the way to impress a lady. He needed to make his declaration more personal. He took the tea-cup from her hand and placed it on the small table to get her full attention, then edged closer to her. "Not to sound like a geeky kid, but that's a big deal for me. Haven't thought about a woman the way I think about you in a long time."

Her gaze lifted ever so slowly, until he captured her stare. "And how is that, Mark, the way you think about me?" Gone was the thoughtful Laurel, in her place the flirty girl he was just getting to know, and especially liked.

He'd played poker enough in the army to know you never gave away your hand. As it stood, he had a lot of crazy mixed-up cards, but he somehow knew if he played them right he might win. One day. If that's what he wanted.

"Besides a lot?" That got a twinge of a smile from her, which always tripped him up.

Could he trust her with his feelings? She seemed to trust him enough to invite him over at this late hour, to take him to a beautifully decorated guest suite, so they could have some privacy. It was damn obvious she trusted him on many levels.

"I think I'm falling for you—" he may just have revealed a card too many "—and to be honest, that's freaking me out."

Her eyes popped open a bit more, and she reached for his face. "I wouldn't want you to freak out about anything on my account." Then she kissed him, and he didn't care if he'd blown his hand or not. "The thing is," she said with a trusting gaze, "I think I'm falling for you, too."

She had his full attention, and the sincerity in those wide, light hazel eyes made her look like a young, delicate-hearted girl. That worried him, yet he was drawn too closely to her in the moment, so he skipped over that "worried" part. Right to his gut reaction.

"Maybe we should test out this liking-each-other theory," she said. It wasn't a question, and it came out breathy and quiet and very, very sexy.

He'd been looking for a sign, or a tell, and she'd just given herself away. Blurted it right out. After a long, thoughtful gaze into the center of his eyes, triggering tiny bolts of lightning along his spine, she glanced toward the elephant in the room. The king-size four-poster bed.

"Did I mention the kids are all asleep?"

Chapter Seven

Mark seemed as shy about getting naked as Laurel felt. Were they ready for this—making love? Her emotions had been on a roller coaster all afternoon, and after all the chaos settled, her one remaining thought had been how special Mark was. He'd taken responsibility for her son's running off, gone after him and brought him home.

She hadn't met such a good man since Alan died—a real man, as her father used to call her husband. She knew better, didn't she? To let her guard down? She had to protect herself for her children's sake. Okay, that was a flat-out excuse, but still partially true. The thing was, Mark possessed the one characteristic she'd always been drawn to. He was trustworthy. Then all those gorgeous "all man" traits came next, which scared the wits out of her. Yet she'd just come this close to begging the man to make love to her. So the question remained, was she ready? All she wanted to do was get lost in his body for a while, to help put the horrors of the day behind her, to forget how lonely she was every day. For that, she was positive she was ready. But more? Not before she cushioned her heart, because she could never go through the torture of losing someone again. Tensing a bit, she worried she was making a mistake to let go with Mark.

He unbuttoned his shirt, then, with that amazing chest on display and those cut abs just beneath, he put a hand on each of her upper arms, with a serious-as-hell expression. "You sure about this?"

No! But her body betrayed her, wanting to be close and comforted, especially after all she'd gone through that afternoon. It had been so long. Couldn't she take this bit of time for herself, just for right now? *Be bold. Go for what you want.* She pulled her top over her head and, in answer to his question about whether or not she was sure about this, whispered, "Yes."

Her reward was a smoldering gaze of appreciation from a man who didn't seem to mind she'd once carried twins and her abs were nonexistent. He moved in, and his warmth enveloped her. And it was exactly where she needed, no, *wanted* to be. With him. Completely.

Tucked safely away in the Gardenia guest room, they kissed and kissed, and he worked her up to near panting. Still, Mark kept his hands strictly above the waist. It gave her pause, and she wondered how long it'd been since he'd been with a woman. Mark would be the only other man she'd ever made love with besides Alan. The thought released a shiver through the heat Mark had done such a great job stoking with his deep kisses and needy caresses. Yet they were still only half-undressed and just halfway to the bed. Besides being the handiest man she'd ever met, he was also a gentleman. *Make it clear that you want him.*

So she stepped things up several notches by reaching between the front of his legs and gently squeezing.

After that he delivered an amazingly ragged kiss, lifted her as she wrapped her thighs around his hips, walked her to the bed, then laid her down. In her excitement, she fought for her breath and let Mark have his way with her neck and breasts. Scattering chills across her shoulders and chest, he explored and kissed the parts bulging above her standard white bra. Her legs remained wrapped around his waist, a deep pulse pounding harder and harder in her core. *Be careful*, an annoying tiny voice far in the back of her mind whispered. She ignored it.

Suddenly needing more to silence her doubts, she cupped his head in her hands and guided his gaze up to hers, first kissing him tenderly on the lips, then reconnecting with those eyes. Silently she communicated, *I'm ready*, at once exciting and frightening her.

With his hair mussed and those heavy-lidded blues knocking her sideways with longing, she could practically hear his reply.

In the next moment, he lifted her again, her legs still wrapped around his hips, pulled back the bedspread and laid her against the supersoft sheets she'd handpicked for guests. Then he removed her bra and lounge-y sweatpants, and peeled down her weekday, nothing-special cotton briefs. Because she didn't have any idea her day would end like this when she'd showered an hour ago. In the next moment, he got rid of his jeans and baby blue boxer briefs.

The sight of Mark Delaney without his shirt or underwear, fully erect, nearly blinded her with desire. The nagging reservations dropped like autumn leaves—she finally and firmly gathered them and tossed them out the window—and the chills ignited in scattershot when he covered her. She felt every part of his tight body. So different from Alan. When Mark rolled over and she wound up on top, his hands cupping her hips snugly against him, sparklers set off beneath every erogenous zone she possessed. As they moved together, slick with heat, powered by passion, she became completely lost in Mark, and the amazing way he made her feel. And how very, *very* lucky she was.

Wednesday afternoon, it was awfully hard to face Peter with memories of Laurel and their Monday love-making night flashing fresh in Mark's mind. But he'd promised another surfing lesson, and because he wanted to build bridges and not tear them down with the kid, he walked Peter to the storage shed with a planned surprise, not caring if the kid saw it as a bribe or not, because it wasn't his motivation.

"First off—" Mark decided to dig right into the conversation they needed to have "—I just want to say I'm not the kind of guy who abandons his friends. And I consider you a friend first, Peter."

Peter found something fascinating with his tire-tread sandals rather than make eye contact.

"Do you believe me?"

"Yes," he said begrudgingly.

"So you've got to understand that if your mother and I like each other, your world isn't coming to an end. That nothing's going to change between you and me. Right?"

"I guess."

"You guess? Is that all you think of me? After all the

time we've spent together, don't you think you can tell if I'm being honest or not?"

Finally Peter glanced up, skipping over Mark's steady gaze and off toward the hotel. "I believe you."

"Good. Now that we've cleared that up, I've got a surprise for you."

Peter's head bobbed quickly back in Mark's direction.

He gave Peter the old surfboard he'd been working on, and his reaction was predictably jazzed. Mark sensed they'd entered a new level of trust and, hopefully, friendship.

To top things off, Peter had his best ride ever that afternoon. They'd hooted and high-fived, and Mark could see new confidence in the kid who'd run off just two short days before.

Thursday, after making love with Laurel a second time just that morning, it was downright awkward stepping in with the twins when Laurel had a meeting with a town historian. Last minute, she'd promised a quick tour of the B&B, and Peter was at the high school library working on a term paper.

Claire and Gracie had a school assignment to gather as many different leaves as they could for an art project the next day. While Laurel gave the B&B tour, Mark took the girls on a walk. They hit the residential area a couple of streets up that was lined with an assortment of trees, including maple. Though the field trip was mostly to get them out from under Laurel's feet, he wanted to do whatever he could to help her build her business.

Because he cared about her? The thought was surprising whenever he had it, but it was true, and he caught a wide smile on his face in a reflection on a parked car window.

Each girl carried a brown paper bag. Gracie piled leaf after leaf in hers, while Claire was more discerning, choosing the biggest or the most colorful. While Claire stood with hands on her hips, making a choice, Gracie put down her bag and found two huge brown and orange maple leaves nearly the size of her head, then ran in circles flapping them in the air.

"I'm pretembering I can fly," she sang.

"She means—" Claire started.

"I got that one, hon. I know what she meant," he said gently with a reassuring smile.

Gracie grinned at him.

Claire pushed her pink glasses up her nose and mumbled "Pretending" anyway.

For different reasons, he wanted to hug both children, which jolted him. Maybe he was getting in way over his head with Laurel and her kids. But he had to admit, standing in the late-afternoon sun, watching them make over leaves like they were the greatest invention on earth, felt kind of good. And he didn't mind—scratch that, liked—he *liked* spending time with the twins. Yikes.

Friday morning, Mark got invited to Laurel's for breakfast. She'd made an incredible egg soufflé, lighter than air, and filled with fresh garden herbs. She planned to serve one for her guests on Saturday morning, and wanted his opinion. They took two bites and made super-satisfied groans to each other, then he fed her a bite and she fed him one. That led to more pleasurable sounds, looking into each other's eyes, and leaving their brains on the back porch, because next thing they knew, they were doing it on the kitchen island.

A half hour later, Laurel had the great idea to try out the modernized, room-enough-for-two bathtub in suite number three. After what they'd done in the kitchen, a bath sounded like a great idea. For fun, Mark picked Laurel up and carried her in his arms up the stairs until halfway up, where he realized he wasn't as strong as he thought.

"Just a second," he said, on the midpoint landing, then hoisted Laurel over his shoulder like a sack of cement and continued up.

She protested but giggled. "I'm not that heavy."

"I know, you're the perfect weight and height and—" He could go on because in his book, she was perfect in every way. But he wasn't sure how she'd feel about him being crazy about her. "—and I'm the one with a problem. I'm not as strong as I like to think."

They'd made it to the top of the stairs. "Which way?" he said, playfully biting her hip, since it was so close to his jaw.

"Ahh!" She giggled more. "Stop that. To the left. Door number two." At least she didn't insist he put her down.

He followed her orders and found his second-favorite room in her B&B. Smaller than the others, but with a skylight that kept the room bright and open, and a bathroom that overlooked the ocean with enough privacy to leave the curtains apart.

He slowed at the foot of the bed. "Want to stop here first?"

She gave an impish glance. "Maybe after the bath?"

"I like the sound of that. Will we have time?" He knew the twins got picked up at noon.

From over his shoulder she checked her watch upside down. "Yes, but you'd better let me down. All the blood is running to my head, and I think with your wicked plans we need to reverse that."

He planted her feet securely on the antique and restored pale blue bathroom tile, then looked at the modern tub taking up nearly a third of the space. He waited for her to get her bearings, made sure she wasn't dizzy, then kissed her bright red face. "I never get tired of kissing you."

She blinked and looked pleased. "We've only been kissing for a few weeks."

"Best few weeks ever." What was wrong with him, acting all crazy about the girl? He could scare her off if he kept this up. Or maybe she liked it.

Instead of chasing her away with his admissions, she settled her palm on his chest. They may not have taken off their clothes in the kitchen, but he'd opened his shirt so he could feel as much of her as possible. Now, the warmth of her hand turned him on as much as if she nibbled his earlobe. But what moved him the most was the way she didn't look directly into his eyes. Instead, she watched her hand slide over his chest and along his side, down to the rim of his jocks. He liked where this was going.

Her lids lifted quickly and she gave a coy smile. His zipper was still down, from their little foray in the kitchen, and as she continued to stare at him, her hand slid beneath the band of his briefs, then around to the back to grab his glute. "Let's get these off you." Seductive, persistent and right to the point. He liked it.

A few simple words, and he sprung to life again. Though in this case her actions spoke louder as she yanked down his jeans and freed him of his underwear.

While the tub got filled, they spent their time wisely, touching, tasting, working each other up for what he was sure would be the best bath of his life.

She directed him into the tub, filled with the perfect temperature of water, then she straddled him. With his head against the cushioned end of a well-planned tub, the view of Laurel's breasts up close and oh so personal, as well as the spectacular ocean over her shoulder, he thought he'd gone to heaven. From the exquisite expression Laurel wore, he was positive he'd brought her along with him.

Soon water was sloshing everywhere, up and over, onto the tile, but they didn't care, because they had a whole lot of other stuff going on. The best lovemaking Mark could ever remember, why? Because he cared about the woman on his lap who took the entire length of him, and gave as much as she took. Tight and deep inside Laurel, bringing her to the brink, was the one place he felt healed and complete. And nothing else mattered.

Several minutes later, after the water settled down, and his heartbeat returned to normal, he held her close to his side and kissed the top of her head. All he wanted to do was hold and protect her. And something more— he wanted to be a man she deserved.

As though she could hear his thoughts, she lifted her face, making close contact with his vision. They didn't say a word to each other, but her nearly fully dilated pupils sent a powerful message. She was as much into him as he was her. Sexually satiated, a tender rush overtook him. He slipped his fingers around the base of her head, his thumb caressing the front of her ear, then drew her near and kissed her with a feeling he could only describe as love pulsing in his heart.

Laurel stopped the kiss, to gaze at him quizzically,

as though she'd felt it, too. As the fine hair on his neck stood on end, her nipples pebbled and gooseflesh covered her chest and shoulders. Something powerful had passed between them. And yeah, whatever it had been, the feeling was mutual.

In silence, they lay in the tub, holding each other, kissing and nuzzling from time to time, until the water cooled. Only one thing bothered him. A drip, drip, dripping. He glanced at the pedestal sink with the antique faucet and saw the source.

"I'll fix that for you," he said.

"I think you could fix everything for me," she whispered against his chest.

The increased and intensifying meetings with Laurel made Saturday morning extra tricky facing Peter. His mother blew Mark's mind, and they couldn't seem to get enough of each other. But the kid had penance to pay, and seeing the gazebo project to the end, as Laurel had put it yesterday morning while naked and tangled up in Mark's body, would help build character.

Yeah, they'd reached the point in their relationship where they talked about all kinds of things after they made love. He hadn't shared so much or so easily with another person of the female persuasion in his entire life. He also got the impression Laurel needed their stream-of-consciousness talks as much as he did. After sex, when they were completely relaxed and intimate with each other, that's when they really opened up.

Mark and Peter touched up the gazebo's white paint, then attached matching bouquet holders on each side of the arched entry. His mother had insisted on it. The morning sun beat down on his shoulders, and he felt alive like he hadn't in several years.

"I brought you some lemonade." His favorite neighbor, Laurel, handed him and Peter each a plastic glass of the best minted lemonade Mark had ever tasted. He knew her guests had to love it, too.

"Thanks," he said, hoping the smoldering gaze he gave Peter's mother went over the kid's head, because, hey, he couldn't help it.

Her shy smile in response was nearly his undoing. Really? He'd seen every inch of her, felt and kissed just about everywhere, too, but right now in front of Peter and the Saturday morning sun, she got shy. He smiled long and happily at her, and she let him look at her the way he wanted.

"You won't believe who I just got off the phone with," she said a few moments later, pride and excitement in her voice.

"The president?" Peter could be witty when he wasn't practicing being a reticent teen, and it always surprised Mark.

He snorted. "Good one."

"*A* president, Mr. Smarty-Pants. Of the historical society." Laurel batted her lashes first at her son, then Mark. If she kept this up, he might have to walk her backward against the fresh paint and kiss her senseless. Because that was what they seemed to do best.

"And?" he said instead.

Her eyes brightened, that enthusiastic expression reminding him of Gracie. "They're adding our B&B to their monthly tours!" One arm shot up like she'd just won the million-dollar lottery, and she looked so damn cute, he wanted to kiss her in the worst way.

"Hey, that's great!" Mark couldn't help himself another moment. He put down his drink and gave her a celebratory hug, swinging her in a circle. And by her reaction, he knew where her twins got their giggles.

"What're we celebrating?" His mother came walking across the lawn, the contagious joy making her smile. Or maybe it was seeing her son laughing and smiling, hugging and twirling a woman like he didn't have a care in the world.

Mark let Laurel explain the good news. Then Maureen hugged her, too. "How wonderful!"

After things settled down, Maureen got a look at the finished gazebo. "Wow, this looks great!" She smiled at Mark and Peter. "You guys did a fantastic job. I can't wait to have our first wedding here." She glanced at Laurel, then clapped her hands. "I have an idea—why don't we all celebrate Laurel's good news tomorrow night. Instead of having dinner in the pub, let's have it out here in the gazebo. We can barbecue. Laurel, bring the kids and we'll picnic outside."

"Sounds great."

But Maureen wasn't finished. Her eyes widened more. "We should work out a wedding package where the couple, who may want a nicer suite than we have to offer, can get married here, by the beautiful sea, then after the reception in The Drumcliffe restaurant, they can walk right across the street to your B&B."

"To start their honeymoon! That's a fabulous idea." Laurel looked amazed and nearly as excited as his mom. "Have you seen my newlywed suite?"

"Not yet."

Laurel slipped her arm through Maureen's and started down the lawn. "Come over and have a look. It's gorgeous and isolated from the other rooms." Laurel smiled at Maureen as they walked arm in arm. "I think you're onto something."

"I know I am."

The sight of Laurel and his mother acting like best friends warmed Mark's chest. She was becoming a part of their little beach community, a part of his family's business and a part of his heart. The thought sat like a cold stone on his chest, yet perspiration appeared above his lip, and the look he shared with Peter could only be described as awkward.

Sunday night Mark stood back, watching Laurel and her kids interacting with his entire family, and, forgetting the hesitation he'd felt the other day, his smile came from deep inside. He'd been asked to grill the chicken, and though they'd planned to eat outside tonight, most of the activity took place farther away on the yard from the built-in patio grill. Still, he watched as Keela and Laurel had an intense conversation about something, probably school-related, while the three little girls played like lifelong friends, chasing Daisy around in circles.

Peter and Sean parked themselves on a picnic bench nearby and discussed The Drumcliffe's and Prescott B&B's websites. Peter's knowledge was impressive. From the look on his father's face, the kid had impressed him, too.

Soon, Mom picked up where she'd left off with Laurel, and announced to the family their big plans for linking their amenities together where wedding packages were concerned. Sean and Peter had a quick follow-up conversation about that, too. How to link the websites together, and how to share photographs of the "wedding" gazebo and the "honeymoon" suite across the street.

He wished he wasn't stuck grilling meat, but enjoyed

seeing Laurel and her kids getting unofficially inducted into the Delaney clan.

Conor came strolling over with a beer in his hand for Mark and a soda for himself, since he was scheduled to work that night. "How're things going between you and Peter?" He lowered his voice to ask, since Dad and Peter were close by.

Mark thanked him for the beer with a nod and took a quick sip. "As good as can be expected. I still don't think he's crazy about my seeing his mom, but he's not complaining. To me at least."

Conor's gaze skipped away to the lady in question across the yard, sitting on a picnic table bench. Currently, Daisy had her front paws on Laurel's knees and was trying her best to lick Laurel's face. She giggled and dodged the inevitable for as long as she could, until the friendly dog's tongue landed smack on her mouth.

"And how're things going with her?" Conor arched his gaze in her direction, rather than be obvious and point at her.

Under his brother's scrutiny, Mark felt his ears heat up. Yeah, he had it bad, and he and Laurel had just started getting to the good stuff. But there was no way he'd admit that to Conor, who'd pester him until he spilled some details. Details that he'd prefer to hoard for himself. "Good, man. Really good." He hoped he'd sounded casual enough.

Conor narrowed one eye. "You dog."

"What?" Suddenly, Mark needed to turn a whole lot of chicken legs and breasts, and wow was he busy.

Then came Grandda. "'Tis a beautiful night. Dinner smells grand. How's the world treatin' my boys?"

"Same old, same old, Grandda," Conor answered first.

Disappointed with Conor's reply, Grandfather threw his attention to Mark. "And you, my boy, need your old grandda to drive you and her—" he tossed his head in the direction that Laurel stood with the other women "—to dinner again?"

It'd been a while since they'd had an official date, mostly because of their schedules and Peter's running away. Mark had been holding off from making waves by taking Laurel out again. Now that his grandfather had mentioned it, the idea was a good one, and he had a special place in mind. "If it would be okay, I might like to borrow the golf cart next time and drive her myself."

"Of course," Padraig said, smiling at Mark, then glancing across the yard to Laurel with her hair blowing in the wind. She wore a sophisticated but simple cream-colored outfit, pants that fit her curves to perfection and a silky top that billowed in the breeze. Even her flats were beige. "She's a good one, Marky."

The heat from the barbecue made Mark's face go red. He fanned the smoke with his hand and tried not to feel the pressure, or let it get in the way of his romance with Laurel.

Dating a woman with children was a challenge, but after the awesome week he'd spent getting to know her in a most intimate way, he thought he might be able to pull it off—getting more and more involved with a lady and her family, and all that went along with it. Which reminded him.

Mark asked Conor to take over for a few minutes, then he approached Peter sitting alone on the nearby bench. Dad had been called into the kitchen by Mom to help with the side dishes, so Mark seized the moment.

He sat beside the teenager. "Thought I'd run something by you."

Peter turned with a questioning glance. "Okay."

"I'd like to ask your mom out to dinner Thursday night. Is that okay with you?"

The boy looked confused followed by thoughtful. "You worried I'll run away again?"

"We're past that, right?"

Peter studied his Vans. "Yeah, I guess so."

Mark had hoped their conversation about moving forward in life since the move had sunk in. But who knew how a teenager thought anymore. It seemed a lifetime ago since Mark had been one.

"Yeah, you guess so, you're over it? Or yeah, you guess it's okay for me to ask your mom out?"

The teen hitched one corner of his mouth and let out a tiny sigh. "You can ask her out," he said begrudgingly.

Peter didn't look at Mark, but Mark thought they'd just cleared a huge hurdle. He gave the kid two firm pats on the shoulder. "Thanks, man. See you at the beach tomorrow at four, right?"

Now Peter glanced at him. "Yeah. I'll be there."

They hadn't even eaten dinner yet, and Mark had already solved one of his problems. Now if he could just get his family to leave him alone.

Later Sunday night, Mark took his grandfather up on his offer to arrange a dinner at a swanky golf club on Thursday night, especially when Grandda offered to watch Laurel's kids. Well, check in on them, anyway, since Peter was perfectly capable of looking out for his sisters. Now all he had to do was ask her. He took out his cell and called.

He and Laurel had been sneaking time together throughout the week. He wasn't being greedy or anything, but he'd been there three times. They used the stolen hours to strip down and drive each other crazy. Always pressed for time, before the girls got out of kindergarten, they rarely had a chance to do normal things like talk. Dinner, just the two of them, at a swanky golf course clubhouse seemed the perfect way to spend a Thursday night, since her weekends were usually booked with B&B guests.

Thursday at 6:00 p.m., he pulled the electric golf cart to her house, hopped out and whistled his way up the steps to her door. The thought of spending the evening with Laurel put him in a terrific mood. He'd borrowed another shirt from Conor, this one gray, and wore a new pair of dark dress pants to fit in at the members-only restaurant. They required jackets, so he'd borrowed one from Daniel. Grandda had been given an honorary lifetime membership there for being one of the original laborers when the golf course had first been designed back in the 1950s, though the family rarely took advantage of it. *It's about time.*

When Laurel opened the B&B door, dressed like a sexy dream in a black sheath, with lots of leg showing and strappy shoes, her hair swept up on her head and wearing dangling sparkling earrings, his first thought was to skip dinner and walk her right back inside, preferably to one of the guest suites they hadn't yet tried.

"Wow, you look phenomenal."

She liked the comment, her face brightening and those sexy lips parting into a smile. "You're looking pretty hot yourself," she whispered. The kids were in the next room, and they didn't need to hear the two of them making over each other. But man, he planned to revisit the subject the first chance he got.

But her smile soon shifted downward. "Thought I should warn you, Peter's being moody."

"Should I talk to him?"

"I don't think it would do any good. Sometimes he just needs to brood. He told me when he closes his eyes, he can't 'see' his dad anymore. His face looks blurry."

"But you've got pictures all over the house."

"Yeah, I mentioned that. I'll talk more to him later." She looked over his shoulder to the golf cart, and an amused expression followed.

Taking her cue that their conversation about Peter and his sad mood was over, he matched her sudden interest with the golf cart. "In keeping with our dating tradition, I thought we'd take the scenic route."

After grabbing some sort of black-and-gold woven shawl and saying her goodbyes, he helped her into the cart. Then he took time to appreciate how her dress rode up her thighs when she sat. He drove the cart down a deserted beach road to a secret entrance to the exclusive golf course in question. A mid-October evening, it was clear, breezy and cool, with a golden tint making everything look beautiful. Especially his date. He took the time to admire her until her eyes widened and he nearly ran up a curb.

Once at the clubhouse, which seriously hadn't been updated since the sixties—all dark colors and leather upholstery—they ordered a drink at the cozy, traditional-styled bar while waiting for their table. It felt great to have Laurel all to himself, but it took tremendous willpower not to undress her with his eyes.

A small jazz trio played quiet music in the corner. The second song in was an old standard, something easy to dance to. Their table wouldn't be ready for a few more minutes, so, to kill time, he did something he hadn't done in over ten years—he asked a woman to dance. And that woman looked very surprised.

He'd never been a great dancer, but he knew how to move a lady around a floor, and she did a fine job of following him. At least he hadn't smashed her toes or anything awkward like that. Yet. Holding her close, looking down into her dreamy hazel eyes—with that romantic old standard played halfway decently by the trio in the background—he became overcome with Laurel.

"You're beautiful," he said. "I can't believe how lucky I am."

Her lashes lifted slowly, her gaze on his, a tender smile creasing her lips. "I thought I was the lucky one."

That did it, he had to kiss her. Right then. Right there on the clubhouse dance floor, he didn't care who saw them.

Be careful. This could turn into a world of pain. Mark's mouth covered Laurel's. Kissing him was like nothing else in her world these days, tender and teasing, sexy and sweet, all wrapped into one glorious package of a man.

The nearness of Mark always made Laurel skip over the scary part, even though she knew she was in way over her head with this fling or whatever she wanted to rationalize calling it. Way over her head.

A couple of hours later, having shared the Thursday special for two—shrimp appetizers, salad, prime rib, baked potato and seasonal vegetables, and a small chocolate molten something or other for dessert—they arrived back at the B&B. They'd laughed and chatted throughout the meal, and underneath the conversation and good food, there was the constant humming of how good she made him feel.

Laurel was no ordinary date. She was special, in all the right ways. He held her back for one moment before they got out of the cart to kiss her.

"I had a great time," she said, her eyes happy and sincere.

"Me, too. Let's go to a movie next time."

"A grown-up movie? Not animated? Wow, it's been ages."

He sat in the cart, the moonlight shimmering over her hair, and he knew he had it bad, really bad, so he kissed her again.

Waltzing through the door and into the family living quarters, they found the girls asleep in bed and Peter in the TV room still up watching some sort of adventure movie, with Grandda's head resting on the couch as he snored.

"What are you still doing up?" Laurel whispered, though the TV was loud enough to wake Padraig up, if that was going to happen. The man was out.

"I didn't want to wake him up," Peter said, motioning to Padraig.

"That's no excuse. You could have left him there and gone to bed."

"But this is a good movie."

"Too bad, you'll just have to record it and watch the rest tomorrow."

While Laurel and Peter continued their heated whisper conversation, Mark noticed a drawing on the table. It was a perfect likeness of his grandfather—slack-jawed and sleeping. He stepped closer and picked it up. "You draw this?"

Though Peter's brows were pushed down while side-tracked arguing with his mother, he nodded.

"This is really good." Mark remembered the day he and Conor were running around looking for Peter when one of the kids in his fifth-period art class said he never missed, and Peter had once told him art was his favorite subject, but Mark had never had evidence until now.

"Thanks."

Laurel had shared earlier about Peter worrying he couldn't visualize his father in his mind anymore. "Ever think about drawing your father's portrait?"

Peter shot a surprised expression, and Mark worried he'd betrayed Laurel's confidential conversation.

"That's a great idea, Peter," Laurel said, easing Mark's concerns.

"Maybe even try painting a portrait after drawing one," Mark said, sensing he was onto something.

Peter still hadn't said anything, but his crinkled brows at least showed he was thinking about the conversation, so Mark continued.

"You know, my mom's a really good painter. Maybe you two can get together sometime. She's got canvases and paints. The whole works. What do you think?"

Though Peter still held back, Mark saw an inkling of interest. "That'd be cool."

"Great," Laurel broke in. "Now it's way past time for bed. Go."

Peter reluctantly set up the record button for the movie and turned off the TV, then started for the bathroom.

"Peter?" Mark called after him.

"Yeah?"

"Okay if I kiss your mother good-night?"

Silence. Then, "I guess." A resigned tone, but progress.

Mark turned to Laurel with a victorious smile. "I got the okay."

She grinned and stepped into his arms, and he proceeded to kiss her soundly good-night—until Grandda woke up with a snort and a sputter.

The two weeks after Peter had run away were like a schoolgirl's dream. Laurel and Mark quickly figured out they had her house to themselves Monday through Thursday in the mornings when the kids were safely in school, and when she didn't have B&B guests. And they took every advantage. They'd tried out each guest bed in the house, except for the honeymoon suite. For some crazy reason, Laurel considered that room sacred, like it belonged only to people who'd made vows. Especially now that she'd be joining forces with The Drumcliffe and their wedding packages.

They also avoided *her* bed, the one she'd shared with Alan for thirteen years. The thought of making love with Mark in her room, on her bed, even though the mattress had been changed, was still more than she could handle.

Mark brought back the wild, early lovemaking days she'd remembered when she'd first met Alan. She'd also transitioned from letting old thoughts come between her and the moments with Mark, to kissing them goodbye. Literally. All over his gorgeous body. Even when sometimes after he left she'd tremble all over thinking she'd opened up too much with him, that if he walked away tomorrow, she'd already feel pain from losing him. It'd happened that fast, right under her nose.

Afraid or not, it was too late, she'd crossed the line, this guy had gotten to her. The scary part about caring and suffering because of it had already occurred.

In other words, where Mark Delaney was concerned, she was already toast.

Last night, "date night," they'd seen a live-action movie with stars she knew, cussing and mature themes. So grown up. Today, Friday— with nearly a full booking for the third weekend in a row, she and Mark didn't dare mess up a bed. She wore a dress, the style Mark really liked, a fitted sheath, and a simple string of fake pearls. In the upstairs alcove, they stood snug watching through the sunlit window as the ocean rolled in and out. Mark breathed gently over her shoulder, his arms wrapped around her waist.

A storm from up north had caused the waves to swell higher. Curl tighter. The sight invigorated her. She turned in Mark's arms to capture his lips, forcing herself not to ask the dumbest question ever—*what are you thinking?*

Why ruin the moment? Their quiet time, holding each other, the tender act of simply enjoying being together. Trusting they were being honest about whatever it was they had going on. *It is what it is.* Wasn't that the popular phrase?

They'd found a secret, the two of them, like a magic balm for their pain. They could make each other feel good, without getting attached. Or at least that was the lie Laurel told herself as their days as a "couple" went along. She was toast.

"I haven't seen waves like that in years," Mark said, obvious awe in his voice.

"They look scary."

"True, but a real challenge." Things went quiet for a few moments as they continued watching the angry water. "You needed something adjusted?" He snapped out of wherever he'd gone mentally.

"Oh, yes, the honeymoon suite windows are stuck. I didn't realize it until I tried to air the room out yesterday."

"Anyone book it yet?"

"Not yet, but I've got to be prepared."

He offered an understanding smile, and, as always, it stirred up feelings she wasn't even ready to name, let alone examine.

Their biggest challenge, since they'd started having sex, was not to react obviously to each other in front of the kids or his family. Which became harder and harder with each passing day. All he had to do was walk in a room and her core tightened with longing. But her feelings went deeper than that, and that, like the big old scary ocean outside, was what frightened her most.

By Sunday morning, the high surf had made all the newspapers, and people came to the beach in droves to watch the breakers thunder onto the shore. Only the craziest surfers took advantage.

After Laurel's last B&B guest checked out, Mark, Laurel and the kids brought chairs and set up on the beach near the lifeguard station. She'd filled a picnic basket so they could all eat a late lunch together and watch the leftover waves from last week's storm roll in.

"Wow, did you feel that?" Laurel said, munching on an egg salad sandwich.

"Felt like an earthquake." Peter had an eerie look in his gaze, like he might not feel safe sitting this close to the water.

"How come they're so big?" Claire yelled over the noise.

"Yeah!" Gracie.

"There was a big storm somewhere and this is the

aftermath," Mark said, realizing the twins probably didn't understand his explanation. Another whitecap pounded the shore. Fighting an unreasonable desire to hit the water with the other hardcore surfers, Mark stayed put, eating corn chips and the egg salad Laurel had made, enjoying the extra-thick homemade wheat bread. He watched the fearless men on the boards wipe out and get pummeled time and time again, not giving up while getting the snot beat out of them.

"Why aren't you out there?" said a man nearby with a distantly familiar face.

"These little things?" Mark laughed at a mere ten-footer. "I'm waiting for the real swells."

The vague acquaintance laughed with him, but he soon became engrossed in a wave that Mark estimated could be twenty to thirty feet, the first of a swelling set in the distance. His pulse leaped to action. Wow. This was epic, once in a lifetime. He stood for a better view. Ten-plus years ago this would have been a dream come true.

With the promise of more of the same from Poseidon, a lone surfer paddled out, putting himself between the whitecaps and the leftover storm. Mark zeroed in as the surfer waited for the next mega breaker heading his way. Then, with perfect timing, he paddled, caught the wave, and surfed through a large, hollow and thick curl of water.

Mark excitedly tapped Peter on the arm. "Look at that! That guy's riding the tube. Wow. You don't see that around here."

Peter stood and cheered the guy on. When the surfer came out the other side unscathed, Mark and Peter high-fived as if they'd just mastered the curl themselves.

Swept up in the moment, it hit Mark suddenly. He

didn't have time to think things through. But he had to try it. Had to. To be out there, feeling the rush of leftover storm in his own backyard. With a seize-the-day attitude, he took off at a run to the hotel, for his board and some trunks, and ten minutes later, hyped up and ready, he was back.

He saw awe in Peter's eyes and horror in Laurel's.

"You're not thinking of trying that are you?" she said an octave higher than her usual voice range.

"YOLO, Mom!" Peter answered for Mark.

You only live once. Key word being *live*. From what Mark had seen, there'd been plenty of wipeouts, but no one had been seriously injured. Why not go for it? Maybe ride the wave of his lifetime. Outside of meeting Laurel, if this opportunity wasn't evidence of things looking up for him, what else could it be?

"I've got to, babe. Trust me." Yeah, he'd slipped up and called her *babe* in front of the kids, and his plea for trust had fallen on unhearing ears. Laurel had moved from shocked to silent in record time. She'd gone inward and didn't kiss him or wish him luck. So focused on the ocean, he ignored that, too, and amped to the max, took off for the water.

"Epic!" he heard Peter say.

After thirty minutes, several attempts and no luck, Mark saw it. The Wave. Had to be over twenty feet high from trough to crest, and promised to give him that ride of his life. He swam the board out, sat and waited, then set himself up, paddled like crazy, caught the deep face of the wave and took off. He'd never experienced anything like this on his board before. A combination of terror and sheer joy set in.

Everything was going great riding the wall, adrenaline ruled the moment and, like a bucking bronco, the

Herculean power of the Poseidon launched him and his board off the water and into the air. Which was incredible. Like he could fly. For a moment. Until on landing he buried the nose of his board into the water and wiped out, face-first.

He'd pearled plenty of times in his surfing career, but never on a wave with the magnitude of a gulf storm. Over and over he tumbled under the water, waves pounding him down, down, down, water rushing up his nose, stealing his breath. Adrenaline keeping him alert. Finally, it dropped him on something hard, knocking his head. He opened his eyes to red billows. Fortunately, there weren't sharks in these parts.

As if in slow motion, the wipeout continued, tossing, battering him, chewing him up and eventually spitting him out on the shore. He struggled to get his bearings, but somehow made it to his feet, having no clue where he or his board was, and not really caring about the board. Then he felt two sets of hands under both of his elbows.

"You okay, man?" one of the lifeguards asked.

Shaken to the core, but not about to let the world know, he fudged. "Yeah, wow, what a ride."

Laurel's heart, like that wave, rose from chest to throat to toes. The sight of Mark getting knocked off his board, going under for what seemed like forever, then showing up on the shore with his head bleeding was her undoing. Seeing him need help, struggle to stand, spiked her rapidly beating heart down to her stomach. She thought she might hurl or pass out, so she sat before she could fall. The overworked lifeguards didn't need two patients.

Peter ran toward Mark, the girls clustered near her.

She had to keep it together for their sake, but she could barely stand. She'd slipped up and fallen for him, hard. She'd ignored the warnings and overlooked the fear, and when she'd tried to be honest with herself, to admit that she'd gotten too involved with him, too soon, she'd brushed it off. Now she paid the price of caring.

Her pulse felt like a machine gun in her neck and chest. Thank God, he was okay. And she wanted to kill him for putting her and the kids through this reckless stunt. Did he not give a damn about her or them?

Walking like a zombie, she followed the crowd, because she had to know he was okay.

His stupid, stupid risk-taking had outed her. Her feelings. Behind her smiles and feigned confidence, she was still very much afraid of what life did to people. She cared for Mark, which she was in no way ready to grapple with. It was too soon after Alan. Now, Mark's rash actions had forced her to face her feelings and fears head-on, before she'd processed who they were together and what they were doing. Her carefree fling had turned into a nightmare right before her eyes. She'd been such a liar to herself.

She glanced ahead at the man lying on the sand, the guy she'd just been forced to admit she loved, thanks to his thoughtlessness. He could have broken his neck out there! Right in front of the kids. Did he even think about that?

They'd all been through enough loss for a lifetime.

On shaky legs, she approached the spot where the lifeguards were tending to his head wound and checking out the rest of his body. Seeing him on the sand—getting butterfly strips applied to the gash above his eyebrow—the pain she'd suffered by losing Alan came rushing back. Panic set in. Feeling scared to death, because she'd dared to open her heart again, she let anger take charge. She knew she could never survive losing anyone she loved, ever again.

And he'd risked his life for fun!

What'd that say about how he'd handle her love?

"He's okay, just some cuts and bruises," one of the lifeguards said, seeing Laurel and her apparent ashen color.

"It's a badge of honor, babe," Mark said, sounding giddy or maybe punchy from the beating he'd just taken.

A hazy red wall circled her. She was so angry she couldn't say a word.

Peter and the girls ran up, the spectacle too hard to resist.

"I'm fine, I'm fine," he answered their questions, sat up to prove it, looking disoriented or dizzy. Laughing. A lunatic. He had to be.

How could she fall for someone who didn't care if he lived or died?

She stood there, hands on her hips, so wrapped up in fear and anger, she was unable to show an ounce of compassion or relief. The damage had been done. Her nervous system had reverted to overload. Her worst memories ever.

His grandfather and mother jogged across the sand. Laurel barely noticed until Padraig spoke. "Are you okay, lad?"

"Mark, what were you thinking?" Maureen scolded.

Her old nemesis had returned. Fear. Now close to a panic attack, she fought the primal sound fighting its way from deep in her belly to her throat. But lost. A wail escaped her lips. She shook her head. The sound quickly turned to a scream.

Mark jumped to his feet and grabbed her. She fought

him. He'd made her like this, he couldn't touch her. From the periphery, she saw her little girls and Peter recoiling. Not because of Mark's accident, but because of her reaction to it. Like the night their father died. She'd lost control, and Mark had to fight her flailing arms before he could wrap his around her and hold her tight and stationary.

She groaned and cried, completely out of control, her nose running as much as her eyes. Unwavering, and so much stronger, he forced her still.

"I'm okay. I'm okay. You're okay. It's going to be okay," he chanted over and over, for what seemed like minutes, until she quit fighting. Whether from exhaustion or his calming effect, she settled down. He'd forced her to.

"Is she okay?" Maureen asked, concern obvious. "Let's have her sit down. Bring her here."

Mark escorted Laurel, shaken to the point of rubber-band legs, to the beach chair. He nearly had to carry her the last few steps. She thudded into the chair and buried her face in her trembling hands. Nowhere near ready to face Mark, or anyone else, she stayed that way for what seemed like minutes. Humiliated on so many levels.

"You shocked her, that's what you did, son," Padraig said, stating the obvious. "What she needs is some good Irish whiskey." The words trailed away as he headed off.

The thought of anything going in her mouth made her gag. Mark stayed by her side rubbing her back, as she shivered and dry-heaved, until finally her body began to put itself back together again. It was then she noticed she was surrounded by a crowd of onlookers. More humiliation. She'd made a spectacle of herself, had probably embarrassed her kids beyond repair.

All because she'd let herself do something she had no business ever doing again—caring for Mark.

Obligation weighed as heavy on her shoulders as the stares from the lookie-loos. She struggled to make her mouth move. "I'm sorry I ruined things," she pleaded to her kids, who stood silent with fearful expressions on their faces.

Grandda was back with whiskey, and she took a swallow, letting it burn down her throat and esophagus. She coughed. Couldn't help it.

The crowd lost interest once she'd quit screaming and yelling, and had already disbursed. Mark was still at her side, stroking her arm, concern so prominent in those blue eyes, she couldn't bear to look at him. She took another swallow of Padraig's magic elixir and began to feel warm and lighter, the nerves letting go of their choke hold. She closed her eyes and drifted, as images of the day Alan died, and the deepest pain she'd ever known, replayed.

Mark had released her demons. She'd fooled herself into thinking this, whatever she had with Mark, was different, or was easier. But losing someone she loved had left a scar so deep it would never heal. Today had forced her to face the fact she'd never be normal in a relationship again.

A minute later, "I'm sorry I ruined things," she whispered, her eyes remaining closed, accepting she couldn't do this again. Fall for someone. Ever.

Laurel's extreme reaction to his accident freaked Mark out. She'd acted like he'd tried to kill himself in front of her and the children. Which, when he thought clearly about his impulse to surf the wild waves, came pretty close to the description. Bonehead! But she'd always seemed so together under pressure. So calm about dealing with life. He'd assumed being a widow at such an early age had taught her how to roll with the punches.

He ran fingers through his wet and sandy hair. He'd messed up. Made a bad decision. And Laurel had completely lost it.

"If anyone ruined the day, it was me, babe. I take full responsibility."

She didn't open her eyes. Nor did she relax.

"Peter? Don't ever think about showing off for a girl," he said, trying to lighten the mood, but failing miserably. "That's what I just did for—" He stopped himself from saying "for your mother," realizing it might open a whole other can of worms—dating was one thing, but the fact they'd become emotionally involved, well, baby steps. Especially after insisting to Peter that they were friends just like he and Peter were friends. So he made an immediate edit to his sentence "—you guys, and look where it got me. Your mother's a nervous wreck on account of me." He turned his attention back to the shattered woman next to him in the beach chair, then dropped to his knees. "I am so, so sorry, Laurel."

His mother had taken off and now came back with a cool compress, placing it on Laurel's forehead. "This might help, dear," she cooed.

Laurel whimpered in reply, while his mother patted Laurel's hand and fussed with a few stray strands of hair around her face.

He felt useless…because the damage had already been done. He couldn't take it back. He'd been careless, and she'd paid.

Having seen her meltdown, and how devastating it was to her kids, Mark was overcome with guilt. On top of the aches and pains, not to mention the humongous headache he had, his stomach roiled. A premonition that he'd done something irreparable sent a deep chill through him.

Laurel shook her head, opened her eyes and sat up, looking like her usual self.

"You okay?" he whispered.

She nodded. "I'm fine. Sorry."

"You don't have anything to be sorry about. This is all on me."

She tried to get up, but needed Mark's help. "Peter," she said, "can you get the picnic basket and, girls, help him gather the plates and food?"

Was she back on track or faking it? Mark knew her well enough to suspect she'd forced herself into mommy mode because she had no other choice. Because of him. Once again, his stomach went sour at the thought of what he'd put her through.

The group walked her back home, his mother and grandfather taking off across the street when they reached the B&B and deposited the beach chairs on the lawn. He guided her up the walkway to the steps. She stopped at the door. "I think I'm going to lie down, if you don't mind," she said, her eyes never finding his.

"You need me to watch the kids?"

"I'll do it," Peter broke in, as though sensing his mother needed time alone. Away from Mark. And making it obvious they were a family and he was the outsider.

"If you need anything, call me, okay?" He said it to Peter, but meant it for Laurel's ears. "I'll be here in a flash."

"Is my mommy okay-oh?" Gracie asked, her voice trembling, as her lower lip quivered.

Mark knelt to answer. "She's shook up. It's my fault. You take good care of her, okay?"

"We will," Claire said, sounding far more confident than her sister.

Some teenager Mark didn't know ran up the walkway. "Sir? They think they found your surfboard."

With that, and a heavy heart, and one hell of a throbbing headache, he left Laurel and her children to themselves, and took off to find a surfboard he'd just as soon never see again. And after that, he needed a bottle of aspirin.

Sometime around seven, Laurel, feeling half human again, had showered and eaten—if two bites counted for a meal—and had gotten the kids settled in. The twins watched an animated movie, and Peter was content playing a video game. Still shaken to the core, but back in control, she texted Mark: Can we talk?

She'd spent a lot of time thinking about what she wanted to say while in the shower, almost running out the hot water heater. Then more before she took a nap.

No sooner had the message been sent than she got his reply: Be right there.

She wished she had another jigger of Padraig's whiskey to give her the confidence to say what needed to be said. Mark was a wonderful man, but today he'd reminded her of the most important lesson of her life.

He tapped on her door, and though she didn't feel anywhere near ready, she opened it and let the man she'd regretted letting her barriers down for come in. With her insides zigzagging to her toes, she led the way to the living room. Now all she had to do was explain it to him. That after tonight she couldn't go on seeing him.

Chapter Eight

Dread threaded through every capillary as Mark sat on the small sofa in the B&B living room. Laurel had made sure there was one cushion between them, which ramped up his regret. He'd pulled one of the dumbest things in his life that afternoon, thinking he could surf the mother of all waves. Nearly got himself killed, too. After the new territory they'd entered the last couple of weeks, he couldn't blame her for being pissed.

"I'm sorry, Laurel. I swear I'll never be that reckless again." He hoped to preempt her.

"It's not that easy. I wish it were." She stared out the window.

Mark followed her line of vision and noticed one of the letters on The Drumcliffe sign had gone out—HOT L—and made a mental note to fix it. How had that slipped by him? Because he'd been too busy falling for Laurel? And why couldn't making up for a stupid stunt be as easy as fixing a broken bulb in order to get back on track with her?

"I've lost so much," she said, absorbed in thought. "Then this afternoon, I could've lost you." It was a statement devoid of feelings, as though after her beachside meltdown, she didn't have any left.

He moved closer, tugged her to his side. "But you didn't."

"That's not the point." When she finally looked at him, there was such sadness in her eyes, all he wanted to do was erase it. Some way, somehow. "In that moment, I *had* lost you. It brought back every horrible memory of watching my husband die. Of seeing my kids suffer along with Alan. Of thinking I'd never be able to live without him. But this time it was you."

Now having an inkling of what he'd set off by being selfish and inconsiderate, the previous dread turned into remorse so deep it sank into his lungs, making it hard to breathe. How horrible of a person was he? "I never meant—"

"It's not the point." She flashed a frustrated glance. "My reaction is. I've still got a huge hole inside me." She shook her head. "I'm not ready—"

He wasn't ready to hear what she might say next, so he intervened. "I'm messed up, too, and I'm not any readier than you are for whatever it is we've discovered. It's just, I thought we were good for each other. I hoped we were helping each other. I thought so, anyway."

Her eyes glistened. "You made me want to move on. I let my guard down and let you in. Then today everything came crashing down when you went under that wave. I realized I'd only put a bandage over my pain. I'm not healed. I can't love again." Tears brimmed and slipped over her cheeks. The sight of her angst stabbed deep in his chest. "I can't love because I can't bear to lose anyone else, and until there is some sort of guarantee that won't happen—" her wet, defeated gaze split his heart "—I can't take the chance."

There was no way he could argue with her logic, after all she'd been through, but feeling adequate or not, he needed to try. Because she'd just as much as said she loved him.

"Laurel, I lost so many people during my tours in the Middle East, I lost count. I know it's not like losing a spouse, but I promised myself I wouldn't forget even one of them. Carrying around that burden kept me from living. That's the guy you met in the beginning. Then you came along and I forgot things when I was with you. I felt light again, smiled, started to enjoy life again. You've helped me in so many ways, I can't begin to explain."

Her brows softened, but he could still see resolve in those eyes. "My letting my guard down with you put me in a horrible place today."

"I was hoping maybe I'd helped you some, too."

"I thought you had. But today I found out I'm not ready to care about anyone else yet. The threat, or fear, or whatever you want to call it, of loss is still too real for me. It's too great for me to overcome. I can't do that again. I can't put my kids through it."

He understood her point. *But I didn't die.* He may as well have, because he'd seen firsthand how she'd suffered from the chance he might've. If he had a better handle on what it was they had going on, maybe he could fight back. But he was as confused and new at this as she was. Until he had a better understanding of what he wanted in life, and where a relationship would fit in, she didn't deserve his inflicting irresponsibility and selfishness on her on a whim. She deserved more. Better. Even so, something made him take one last stab at making things right.

"There's no guarantee for anything in life. The only way to avoid loss is to never feel. To hide out. Be a by-stander. I thought that was what I wanted until I met you. So now I'm asking, is that what you want? For the rest of your life?"

A long, strained silence ensued. He was hell bound to leave without an answer. Until recently, he'd been the master of passivity, but Laurel had helped him want to change. Not that he had, but at least he wanted to. He'd hoped he'd done the same for her. Thought maybe he had.

She stared straight ahead, not trying to engage with him. "I can't do it, Mark, I'm sorry. I'm not ready."

Evidently, he hadn't done the same for her.

"My grandfather always talks about the silver lining after our struggles and troubles. Will you at least consider that?"

That drew a quick, rye laugh. "I've fallen for the silver lining bit before, after Alan's remission. I believed it would last. Knew it would, because it had to. We had three kids. I'd believed with all my heart that our nightmares were over—only to find two years later that he'd relapsed."

"I can only imagine what you've been through, all of you."

There was no arguing the point. If she wasn't ready to live, he couldn't force her—that was another thing he knew firsthand. So he did the only thing he could. He stood and, respecting her wishes, prepared to leave the best surprise he'd found in years. The beautiful B&B

lady, who happened to live across the street. "I'm sorry about today, but I understand your decision."

Before he closed the front door, he thought he heard her crying. Torn between running back and comforting her or leaving because she'd asked him to, he honored her request.

Mark walked into his room and found Conor home, sitting on the couch watching sports news.

"You got a minute to talk?"

Inquisitive blue eyes flashed from the TV screen to his. "Sure, what's up?"

"Besides the fact I blew the best thing I've ever had today?" Mark had been changing since getting involved with Laurel, and this was further proof. Instead of shutting down or going off by himself to brood, he was glad his brother was around to talk to. "Did you hear about it?"

"I was working. Does it have anything to do with that bandage on your head?"

"Yeah, I thought I was still a kid and decided to try surfing those crazy waves today. Almost got myself killed. Right in front of Laurel and the kids."

"That's not good."

"Nope. And it didn't go over well. Evidently, I put her in shock, and now she doesn't want to see me anymore."

"You've got it bad for her, don't you?"

"Man, I didn't think I had it in me anymore, but I do. I want to be with her. But I don't have anything to offer, and now she's kicked me to the curb, so what does it matter?"

"Quit shortchanging yourself."

"Dude, I'm a fix-it guy, a handyman."

"Who could run a hotel if he wanted to."

Mark plopped on the adjacent couch and faced Conor, who clicked off the TV. "That's the thing, I didn't think I wanted to. I didn't want the pressure or to have to make decisions. But lately I keep getting ideas about how to do things better, more efficiently around here. I don't dare say anything to Dad or Mom because they'd just encourage it."

"You've always been an organizer."

"What?"

"You started the surf club in high school. And remember when we were kids and you talked Daniel and me into convincing Mom and Dad to take us to Hawaii? You got all those travel brochures and wrote up a presentation for us to give. You covered every angle, and they bought it."

Mark smiled remembering the confident kid he'd been back then. "That was a great vacation, too."

Conor laughed. "It was, and it would never have happened if you hadn't come up with ways for all of us to save money for it. That trip was because of you, brother."

A crazy image of his grandfather wearing a colorful Hawaiian shirt with equally loud golf shorts made him laugh, too. Just as quickly, he remembered how he'd been a platoon leader in the army because of his organizational skills, and how one of his decisions had put his unit in peril. How they'd taken fire for it and lost people. His decision had cost lives.

As if reading his mind, Conor leaned forward, an earnest expression in his gaze. "I know you went through some shit in that sandbox over there, man, and you came home changed. But lately you've started acting like your old self again, and I'm glad. I missed you.

You're not meant to hide out doing chores for the hotel. You've got what it takes to run this place."

He didn't want to hear it, but he also couldn't deny that lately all kinds of ideas had been popping into his head about The Drumcliffe. Being with Laurel and seeing all of the fine touches she put into her B&B had inspired plans of his own.

"What if I fail?"

"Dude, this place has been around so long, it could run itself. All you have to do is try. I think you're ready for it. And maybe it's because of Laurel, or maybe it's because you've finally gotten tired of being a slacker. That really never suited you, man. The point is, whatever the reason, it's time. Step up. You can do it."

Mark wished he had one-tenth the confidence in himself Conor had for him. "I'll think about it."

He'd meant to boo-hoo on Conor's shoulder about Laurel breaking up with him, but something had taken over their conversation and sent it in a completely different direction.

Maybe every messed-up and confusing thing that had happened today right up to this talk with his brother had happened for a reason. Maybe it was time to step up. For himself. For his parents. For Laurel…if she ever gave him a chance again.

By now his head was spinning and he couldn't bear to think of one more thing, so he thanked his brother for the talk, excused himself and went to bed.

Sunday night, a week later, the family dinner may have been more subdued than usual, but Mark had been doing a lot of soul searching and planned a surprise for his parents. He knew he looked as bad as he felt, having stayed awake nearly every night that week, thinking.

Once he told them his conclusion, they might assume he was off his nut, too.

Part of the reason he didn't have a comeback with Laurel that night was because he still didn't know where he was going. Until now he'd been holding out for some reason to take off, to escape the responsibility of the future of the family hotel. But over the past week, after seeing what he'd blown with Laurel, wanting it back more than anything in the world, something changed. He was ready to step up for the family, take on some real responsibility, prove he was a man who could be trusted.

"Mom and Dad, I just wanted you to know I'm ready for you guys to start transitioning to your retirement."

He thought his mother might fall off her chair, and for the first time in ages, he spotted a flash of pride in his father's eyes. "Any way you want to work this, we're on board, son," his father said.

"You can have as much on-the-job training as you need," his mother added. "We can start as soon as you'd like."

"Okay, then. Let's sit down with the reservation software and hotel budget a couple hours every morning starting tomorrow, and for however long it takes until I get the hang of it." That might help keep his mind off the way he'd been spending the best mornings of his life for the last few weeks with Laurel, too.

Nothing short of surprise brought a broad grin to his father's face. "You're on. For as long as you need."

"Well, that's the best news I've heard since the boys in green beat Scotland in 2015!" Grandda announced with glee.

Then they all shook on it, and Mark realized he'd officially changed. Whether Laurel wanted to be in his life right now or not, she'd helped him get here. Never

one for being an optimist, he held on to the hope that
Laurel might see how he'd impacted her outlook on life,
too. Hopefully it would be enough to keep the door open
between them, just enough.

Mark didn't let the breakup with Laurel keep him
from Peter's surf lessons, either. Each Monday and
Wednesday at 4:00 p.m. since the breakup, he met him
at the beach, surprised that Laurel still let Peter come.
At least she trusted him with something.

"Mom's been really sad," Peter said, while they
waited in the water for a wave decent enough to ride.

It'd been two weeks. "The way to help her is to
be there for her. Do stuff without her having to ask.
Offer to watch the twins while she does the weekend
brunches. You know, things like that."

"I don't understand why she got so mad at you."

"I was stupid. Listen, one day you'll have a girl you
like break up with you for something stupid you've
done. It's inevitable."

"Why?"

"We guys can't help it."

Peter laughed, and it helped lighten Mark's mood,
but only for the moment.

"You said that you were friends with my mom like
you were friends with me," Peter said, earnest as hell.
"I knew that wasn't true."

They stared at each other, Mark seeing a kid who
needed his "friend" to be straight with him.

"I'll be honest, I like your mother in a whole different
way. Have from the beginning. That's also something
you'll figure out real soon for yourself."

Things went quiet, and they watched for a wave with
possibilities. The moments stretched on.

"Hey, how would you like a part-time job helping with surfing lessons for hotel guests? It wouldn't necessarily be regular work, it would depend on whether people signed up for it or not. You could be my assistant. What do you think?"

"You want me to help you?"

"You're the perfect choice. You're my friend and you can give the beginner perspective on things. I thought you might want to earn a little cash, in case there's a girl you'd like to buy ice cream for or take to the movies. You in?"

Peter's amazed expression said it all. "Sure."

"Okay, then. I'll let you know over the next few weeks what we set up."

"Okay. Oh, and just so you know, I'm not naive like you think. After I thought about it for a while, I was glad you liked my mom *that way,*" Peter finally said.

Surprised, Mark gave the kid a skeptical stare. "Really?"

"I could tell she liked you a lot. You made her happy. I liked seeing her happy."

Peter's simple comments meant the world to Mark because it gave proof that he'd made Laurel happy, before he'd made his ridiculous mistake. "Except now I've made her really sad and angry."

"Yeah."

The facts were the facts. Even a fourteen-year-old could see that.

Needing a change in topic, Mark glanced over his shoulder and saw that wave with possibilities. Nothing huge, but completely adequate for Peter's novice abilities. "Let's take this one."

Peter saw the swell rising and flashed Mark an elated grin. "Let's do this!"

Later, when they walked home together, each with a board under his arm, Mark patted Peter on the shoulder when they parted ways. The kid smiled. "I'm gonna tell my mom you said hello."

It was Mark's turn to grin. "You do that," he said, heading off to his hotel room, thinking it couldn't hurt to have Laurel's son on his side.

A week later, on the first-ever Historical Society house tour, Sunday afternoon, there was a mishap at the Prescott B&B. Along with the leftover storm waves a couple of weeks back came damper weather. A second-floor door stuck so hard, Laurel had to use her shoulder and hip to shove it open. Not the impression she'd hoped to make.

"As you may know, this is part of dealing with a hundred-and-fifty-year-old house. It's always a good idea to have a handyman on staff." Which made her think about Mark for the thousandth time since she'd sent him out of her life. Not in his fix-it-guy mode, no, but for the great guy he was. The one who made her feel again. After that, she struggled to keep her train of thought.

During the rest of the tour, several other minor but annoying issues made themselves known. A chandelier flickered on and off, one particularly squeaky floorboard every single guest managed to walk over, a constant leak in the antique pedestal sink faucet of suite number three, the very one Mark had promised to fix the day they'd tried out the bathtub. Her face flushed with that memory. What couple would want to listen to that all night on a lovers' getaway?

Her mind went directly to Mark again. If they'd ever had a chance to spend the night together, they certainly

wouldn't use it to sleep. But if they happened to be in
that room, he would know exactly how to fix the of-
fense. She liked that he was practical in one respect and
impractical on the personal side, and sexy as hell. But
more, too. Tender. Kind. Patient with her kids. Peter's
self-esteem had doubled since getting surf lessons and
learning how to build stuff and paint things, as Peter
himself described what he'd learned from their new
neighbor. And living with Peter had been easier lately,
with him brooding less and drawing more. She'd even
caught him playing Candy Land with the girls the other
night while she checked in a couple and gave them a
quick tour of the B&B. The girls had also learned to
pipe down whenever she got a phone call on the reservation line, thanks to Peter giving them the high sign—a
finger over the lips as he coerced them down the hall.
The kid was stepping up and taking some responsibility since working for Mark.

For the last two weeks, she'd felt lost at sea, tossed
by the waves, helpless, alone. Why? Because she'd
banished Mark from her life. Because she was afraid.
Afraid of feeling. Afraid of losing. That was no way to
live. What about the silver lining? It had to exist.

She'd taken back some control in her life by buying the B&B and getting her business up and running.
She'd enrolled her kids in new schools, and other than
the running-away incident with Peter, she'd kept them
safe and fed. The twins seemed ridiculously happy with
their new bedroom and with going to school, and their
new best friend, Anna. They'd be five soon. Growing
up fast.

Peter was working on being less glum and his anger
management had improved so much, a huge part of it
due to hanging out with Mark. He even seemed to be

making friends his own age. Along with developing an unlikely friendship with Maureen Delaney, over their mutual love of drawing and her giving Peter painting lessons with the special portrait of his father in progress. Again, thanks to Mark.

Laurel took a load of bedding to the laundry chute at the end of the second-floor hall, went to the next guest room, stripped the beds and repeated the walk to the chute. When the sheets and towels were all removed, she took the stairs down to the laundry room just off the kitchen to start the wash. On the way, she passed a window and caught sight of Mark. She stopped and watched as he directed a gardener where to trim some bushes and trees. It occurred to her that he used to do that himself, but she hadn't seen him out and around the hotel like she used to.

After Mark finished talking with the gardener, he went inside the hotel office, and only then did Laurel notice he was dressed nicer than usual, like when he'd taken her on their dates. It made her wonder what might be going on with him. It also created a pang of regret and pain in her stomach.

She'd broken up with him because of what she'd been through with Alan. That wasn't exactly fair.

It was time for Laurel to change. To quit letting fear and loss rule her world. Of course, it would be scary to open up to love and loss again, and yes, it wasn't just about her anymore. Not like when she'd first met Alan, and had only herself to think about. She had children to consider now. Children who'd all been through as much loss as she had, who'd experienced more sadness than any kid should have to already. Yet the girls were blossoming and Peter was coping better than he ever had since he'd lost his dad.

If life was all about moving forward, where was she? Stuck in a rut. Part of her couldn't believe she'd ever have to go through the kind of pain and loss she already had ever again. Life should be only a smooth ride from here on out, right? But the other part couldn't let go of the old helpless freefall into widowhood, the part that fought for her husband's life to the very end, then couldn't believe he was gone and would never see his children grow up. That part had ached so deeply for Alan, had grieved to the point of numbness, that it'd become a habit. Along with fear of ever going through that again.

So the question was, did she want to let those sad old habits control the rest of her life, or should she give the "smooth ride" theory a shot?

She shoved as much laundry as she could into the washer and set the controls, then went to the kitchen to figure out what to have for lunch.

She hadn't moved here expecting to meet a man, yet practically the very day she'd arrived, he'd dropped into her life to help. To make things better, and to slowly but steadily pry open her heart again. Maybe Padraig Delaney, with his silly selkie theory, had the right idea. Maybe they were meant to meet each other and fall in love. Because that was the real problem, a much greater issue than his making a stupid decision to ride a wave and possibly break his neck. Nope. The trouble was her fear of loving again. With Mark, she'd started to feel unmistakably like the young girl who'd met and fallen head over heels for Alan. Who'd walked on air when he'd told her he loved her. She and Mark may have been working up to that point, but she'd nipped it in the bud. She'd hid behind a self-righteous decision that she couldn't trust him because he'd made a huge mistake, potentially risking his life. Yet she'd asked him to stand on ladders and crawl onto her roof to fix things with little concern, when he could have gotten injured just as easily at her B&B. She'd trusted him to be careful. Then, at the beach, he wasn't.

Was it fair to punish him, when he'd obviously learned his lesson and had the forehead scar to prove it? In punishing him, she was also punishing herself, and the kids. They all missed him. Sure Peter still surfed with him, but they'd all gotten used to Mark having dinner with them a few times a week. And she'd gotten used to a heck of a lot more.

After a quick sandwich and glass of lemonade, she went back to her chores. Finishing the laundry, cleaning the guest suites.

It was crazy how hard it had become to clean the upstairs suites. To put fresh linen on the beds she'd made love on with Mark. The reminders made her body ache for him, but her pride kept him away.

She thought about the man she'd just seen delegating work instead of doing it himself, then dressed for success, heading inside for who knew what.

Mark seemed so right for her *and* the kids. Her fear had shut him out, and she'd missed him so much for the past two weeks, she could barely take it. Well, maybe it was her turn to learn a lesson and make some changes.

Yet it wasn't that easy anymore. She had to consider her babies.

She walked back down the stairs to Gracie and Claire's room, opened the door, then went across the hall to Peter's, knocked and did the same.

"We need to have a family meeting," she said standing in the middle. "Be in the kitchen in ten minutes. Girls, that gives you both time to use the potty, and

Peter, put on some clothes. Preferably ones that don't smell."

Then she went to the kitchen to pour everyone a glass of lemonade, and to figure out the best way to explain her problem of the heart to her kids.

She also set out a plate of cookies to butter them up.

Ten minutes later, with all eyes on her, Laurel leaned her elbows and forearms on the kitchen island, took a swig of lemonade and went for broke.

"So you've all noticed that Mark doesn't come around here anymore."

"Why not?" Gracie asked.

"I'm gonna get to that. When he got hurt that day at the beach and I was all upset, I asked him to stay away." She took a peanut butter cookie and nibbled a tasteless bite. "And now I miss him."

"I miss him, too." Gracie seemed all into the family meeting, sitting on her stool, looking serious.

"Me, too." Claire pushed her glasses up her nose, then took a second cookie.

"So my question is, if I asked him to come back, and he wasn't mad at me and wanted to hang out with all of us again, would that be okay with you guys? Would it be okay for Mark to be involved in our lives in maybe a more permanent way? That is, if he wants to."

"Yes!" Gracie was first to chime in. "What does perm-ma-mint mean?"

Close. It occurred to Laurel that since the district speech therapist had been working with Gracie for an hour once a week, that her language had improved.

"Forever and ever," Claire, said, snatching another bite and sitting straighter.

How did Claire know that? Both her girls were growing up.

Also, put like that, the thought gave Laurel pause. A mild wave of fear trickled through her, but nothing she couldn't handle. "Well, that's kind of right, I guess. So is that a yes from you, too?"

Claire nodded while making crunching sounds.

So far Peter either abstained or was thinking. She'd wait a few seconds more to see what he thought and how he felt about it. Because, if Peter didn't want Mark around, she'd have some extra discussions to conduct, with him alone. Maybe he wanted Mark to himself, as his friend, and she'd have to help him see and understand the bigger picture. Her children and their feelings would always come first, but there were also times, like now with Mark, where life should be negotiated.

She drank some lemonade and remembered a magazine article she'd happened to read recently, waiting in line at the market, about divorced women starting new relationships. It had emphasized that a woman's personal life and dating shouldn't be put up for a vote. It was personal business, and the woman deserved a life of her own. But that was just a magazine article, and she was a widow, not divorced, and these were her kids. All she had in the world.

"And you, Peter?"

"Mark's my friend, Mom. I see him all the time."

Yup, just what she'd expected. Peter wanted to keep Mark to himself. Okay. That changed things.

"And he seems sad about your telling him to stay away," Peter went on. "And you seem miserable." He took a long draw on his lemonade. "So if it makes both of you happy, I say yes."

When did Peter become so observant and philosophical? She suppressed a smile and the desire to hug him, but let the pride ripple through her for a second or two. Her son was growing up.

"I think it's pretty obvious I've been stuck in a rut, and I'm not sure how to go about it—you know, inviting him back."

"Make him cookies!" Gracie was on her game.

"The chocolate ones," Claire added.

"You're the one who sent him away," Peter said, on his third peanut butter cookie. "And because he's a cool guy and respects you, he's stayed away."

Clearly, she did not know this young man. "Do you know that for a fact?"

"I know him. He's a good guy. So it's up to you to invite him back." Peter glanced around the kitchen, toward the family dining table. "Have him over for dinner, with all of us. Then we'll all go to our rooms so you can talk to him alone."

Why hadn't she thought of that? "Well, that's certainly a good suggestion. I'm just a little nervous about falling on my face in front of you kids, if he wants nothing more to do with me."

"He *loves* you," Gracie piped up again.

"How do you know?" Laurel was fascinated with the girl's blossoming right before her eyes.

"When he sees you, he looks like Daisy when she sees Anna," Claire clarified.

"And Daisy *licks* Anna's face all the time." Gracie got the giggles, and Claire joined in.

Face licking? She'd thought they'd been discreet. How much had her daughters seen of her and Mark kissing? Her cheeks went warm, but she loved how the family meeting was going so far.

Truth was, she couldn't be a good example to her son and daughters if she let fear rule her life by cowering and not going after what she wanted. She'd wanted to make them proud with the B&B, and it hadn't been easy. But Mark was different. He was a person, not a building. She wanted a relationship with him, and that took two people to agree. It was a risk to ask him back into her life, and he may not want to come back.

"So now that you have our support, how are you going to bring him back?" Peter asked, leaning in, looking more like a junior lawyer than her previous temperamental son.

She wanted to burst into tears thinking that one day they'd all be grown and leave...and she'd be alone. Is that what she wanted for her life, to give it all to the kids and forget about herself?

"Good question, Peter." It seemed like it was now her duty to go after what she wanted, as an example for her children. She was an adult, right? So why did she still need backup? She finished her cookie and took another drink of lemonade, deep in thought.

"Okay, here's my plan..."

Chapter Nine

Sunday morning, Mark took a good long look in the mirror while he shaved. He'd quit walking around with a two-day growth since he was stepping up to more responsibility with the hotel. May as well look the part, even if he didn't feel it yet.

Before, with Laurel and the kids, life was chaotic. Now, on his own, it was merely a challenge. But he was willing to power through, to learn the ins and outs of the business. His parents deserved their retirement. As he shaved, he thought about the day Peter asked him to show him how. The kid still had peach fuzz, but they'd borrowed one of Laurel's disposable blades and he'd given Peter a lesson with shaving cream and all.

He'd felt a lot more alive when he was involved in Laurel's hectic life. Something else occurred to him—he wanted that back. He wanted her most of all. Yeah, he'd scared Laurel with his surfing stunt, and she couldn't handle it. Remembering what she'd been through, losing a husband to cancer, with three children to look after, he completely understood her reasoning. But at this point, two years later, was she using that as an excuse? Maybe the real fear was about opening her heart to someone new. But was he the guy? The right guy for her?

He tilted his chin up and shaved his neck, then used a warm face cloth to wash away the excess shaving cream. Maybe she'd given him a huge clue without realizing it? She must care about him or she wouldn't have gotten so upset when he'd gotten hurt that day. The question was, did she care about him in the same way he'd finally admitted he did for her?

He'd taken the first step in changing his position in life, being willing to take on running the hotel and becoming responsible for the business. Wasn't it time he went after what he wanted in his personal life, too? All he had to do was figure out how to convince Laurel that they had a good thing going on, and they should stick with it. Who knew what they might have together?

He looked at himself in the mirror again, looked hard and swallowed slowly. It was time to admit it— he wanted her *and* her three kids. The whole package. That was the kicker. And it scared him. He couldn't just find a woman and tiptoe back into getting involved over time. No, he had to go and pick one with a family. But he'd never done things the easy way.

He wiped his entire face with the cloth, realizing he'd do whatever it took to convince her he was the right guy. When the cloth came down, he smiled in the mirror. Decision made.

"You can quit admiring yourself for now," Grandda

said, appearing from thin air. "We've got a big problem in the boiler room."

Shifting gears from hotelier with an agenda back to fix-it guy, he threw on his T-shirt. Forced to push back his plans to confront Laurel, Mark rushed out the door after his grandfather, heading for the basement.

Laurel gathered all her existing nerves, the long list of needed repairs Peter had suggested she use as the excuse to confront Mark in one hand, and her backup in the other hand. The twins. Gracie was linked between her and Claire. Because, how could Mark resist her adorable girls? She'd also worn the sundress he especially liked the night Peter caught them kissing on the deck of the pub for added effect. With that and a batch of butterflies winging around her insides, they headed for The Drumcliffe.

Entering the lobby of the hotel, she spotted Maureen behind the check-in desk. When she looked up, she immediately smiled. "Hi! What can I do for you?"

"I'm looking for Mark."

"We want to talk to him," Claire said, businesslike and so grown up.

"We *need* him." Gracie went a bit further, and Laurel gently squeezed her fingers. "Ouch." She looked at her sister, who'd evidently done the same, but probably harder.

Embracing the importance of the situation—everyone seemed to know about the breakup—Maureen gave a serious nod to the little ones. "He's in the basement fixing a pipe. We sprung a leak this morning."

"Oh, maybe this isn't such a good time—" After all it took to work up the nerve to come over, Laurel was struck by disappointment. She'd been handed a chance to postpone facing Mark. But she really did want to get this over with, to admit she'd overreacted and wanted a second chance. Hopefully he still did, too. Since she'd made up her mind, every second before facing him seemed like an hour.

"No, I'm sure he'd like to see you. Take that elevator—" she pointed down the hall to the end "—to the basement, then turn right to the boiler room. He should be there."

Today was the day, no squirming out of it. The butterflies were running out of space inside.

A couple of minutes later they followed the noise and found the boiler room, peeked around the door and saw Mark. Now her breathing needed prompting. *Take a breath, blow it out.* He was wearing goggles, using an air hammer and some kind of tool to cut an old, corroded-looking pipe above the water drum. Grandda looked on. A blaring machine-gun-like sound made the girls cover their ears, and didn't help Laurel's hammering heart a bit. It was hot like a sauna in the close quarters, but she couldn't back down now. She had the girls stand behind her skirt as they stood near the exit, in case there was any danger of stuff flying, and waited to be noticed. Which Grandda did immediately.

"We're almost done here," he yelled, as if he was working just as hard as Mark. Then when the racket had ended with the metal cut made, he tapped Mark on the shoulder. "You've got company," he yelled, even though the sound had diminished.

Mark turned, obviously surprised by Laurel and the girls in the hotel boiler room. "Hey, is everything all right?" he said, dropping the tools and standing from his squat, while removing the protective glasses.

The spotlight was on her, and she couldn't even swallow. How could she talk? By sheer willpower. "Actu-

ally, no, everything isn't all right. But you look busy—"
she could feel it coming…the cave "—so I'll come back
later."

"We're halfway done here, but I can take a quick
break. What do you need?"

She'd memorized a short speech on the way over,
and, ready or not, now was the time to use it. Because
it would never get easier to say what she needed to. "I'm
here because I need you," she said as her lips betrayed
her by trembling, as did her hand holding the list. Dang
thing was shaking so much, she wadded it up and hid
it behind her back.

He stared her down, while processing what she'd
said. "You need me." He repeated her loaded words as
if he hadn't heard her right.

There was no hiding now, and her backup team was
staring at her, waiting for their mother to fix things. She
nodded, feeling excruciatingly awkward.

"What's that?" He stared in the direction of the hand
she'd just tried to hide.

"A list."

He motioned for her to hand him the paper.

She did, though she couldn't will her hand to stop
shaking. "It's a list of all the little things that need repair since you haven't been coming around."

"Oh." He looked disappointed. "So when you said
you 'needed' me, you meant in the fix-it way." He
glanced at Claire and Gracie and smiled.

"Hi," Gracie said.

"Hi, kiddos."

Laurel wanted to explain that she needed him in a
hundred different ways, too, but now wasn't ideal, near
a boiler room with Grandda hanging around, so she kept
quiet. Kicking herself for backing down.

When he took the list, their fingers touched, and the reaction was so intense, Laurel almost jumped back. He unwadded it and glanced over the words, keeping a business-only expression in place. "I've got to finish this and clean up, but I'll come over as soon as I can."

She still felt him, where they'd touched, like a lingering low-level electrical shock. She'd missed his touch more than she thought.

"Okay. Thanks. We'll go home, then, and—" she glanced at her flats because it was easier than getting caught up in his steady gaze "—wait." Did she have to sound so desperate on the "wait" part? "Take your time."

This wasn't life or death, it just felt like it.

He was onto her, she could tell by that sweet expression and understanding smile. "Give me about an hour."

Gah, an hour would be equal to eternity.

Mark watched Laurel and the girls leave, Gracie turning back and giving him a wave. Claire walking tall and proud like her mother. A sensation that could only be described as love overpowered him. She'd come here, list in hand, admitting that she needed him. He'd seen the evidence of her fear in the tremble of her lip and the shaky paper. It hadn't been easy. He didn't doubt for one instant that she wasn't sincere. Why else would she bring her girls?

Maybe Peter wasn't around to watch them? Even so, they were witnesses to their mother needing help.

She looked as beautiful as ever, and it was all he could do not to take her in his arms. Who cares who saw? But he wanted to do this right, this making-up and moving-forward business. He was filthy with plumber's grease and dirty water, and he needed to finish the hotel project before he could move on to the most important job in the world. Winning Laurel back.

His plan was to clean up, look his best. Make sure she knew how much he'd missed her, then state his case about "them" being right for each other. Not just right, either. Perfect. They were perfect for each other and if she needed evidence, he'd make a list for her, too.

He'd seen the questions in her eyes, like he was torturing her by not dropping what he was doing and running after her. He understood how hard this had to be for her. Hell, he'd nearly dropped the air hammer when he'd seen her. But he wanted things to be right when he told her how he felt, and from the looks of her anxious expression and trembling hands, she had something more than a to-do list on her mind, too.

Mark showed up at Laurel's an hour to the minute later. He'd showered and changed into a clean pair of jeans and one of his newer T-shirts. She answered the door, quieter than usual, but with a thoughtful smile on her face. How he'd missed those hazel eyes with their golden flecks and hints of green, and those bee-stung lips, which he noticed bore a light shade of lipstick. She wore some kind of loose black lounge pants and a thin purple fleece pullover.

"Get the problem fixed?"

He'd missed hearing her voice, too.

"Yeah, had to replace one of the old boiler tubes above the water drum. Was only the second time I'd done it, so Grandda was talking me through it. The hotel seriously needs a plumbing update, but until business picks up, we'll just have to keep fixing and patching." This mundane stuff was so not what he wanted to be talking about, but he couldn't just dive into the topic of the rest of their lives.

"I hear you on the business-picking-up part." Her nervous hands, wringing and unwringing fingers, were her tell. He tried to ignore them. "I'm going to have to open up Thursday nights if I want to break even. It's a good thing I have Alan's other life insurance policy as backup."

Small talk was going to rule the day, unless he took charge. First, though, he had to figure out what Laurel needed, really needed, from him. He didn't want to go the whole "we're meant to be together" bit if all she actually wanted was a few small repairs to her B&B. How embarrassing that'd be, but he figured he owed her that much for the emotional distress he'd put her through.

He produced the seriously creased list from his back pocket, deciding to go all business. "So, I see from the list you have some tricky lighting issues, a leaky faucet." He paused to catch those caramel eyes flitting around his body and finally landing on his face. "This wouldn't happen to be *the* leaky faucet I noticed a couple weeks ago, would it?"

That halted her for an instant. "That would be the one." A mild flush on her cheeks let him know she, too, remembered what'd gone on in that bathroom before he'd noticed the leak.

So this was how it was going to work. He'd actually have to do some repairs before he could have "the" conversation he really wanted. "Since plumbing seems to be the theme of the day, I'll start there." He carried his toolbox past Laurel, and couldn't help but notice how uptight she seemed as he passed. Was she afraid he was going to grab her or something? That was the last thing he wanted to do to her, make her nervous. He decided he'd get right to work and give her a chance to get used to him being there. Then maybe she'd calm down and relax enough to talk. Because talk they would, before he left today.

Surprisingly, she followed him up the stairs to suite number three's bathroom, and though she didn't talk, she hovered around him while he got set up and went to work. He had to admit her nervous energy was amusing as she flitted about pretending to be busy in the adjacent guest room. She picked this up, moved that, smoothed out the duvet, all while keeping close watch over him. He had excellent peripheral vision. Was she searching for the best way to say what was really on her mind? She was the one who'd come to him. There had to be a reason.

At some point, when he was concentrating on the job at hand, Laurel left, and later, he was just cleaning up around the faucet on the pedestal sink when she reappeared with lemonade and a plate of chocolate cookies. Always a good sign. He couldn't hide his smile, or the direct question that just popped into his head. "Where're the kids?"

With a sly smile, like the Pied Piper, she led him out of the bathroom and into the hall to the window seat. She set the drink and cookies on the small antique table there, then sat. Slowly, she lifted her shapely brows, a cue for Mark to take a seat, too. Which he did, right next to her. Now he could smell that fresh-out-of-the-shower, flowery lotion she used. Yeah, he'd missed that, too. Big-time.

"Peter offered to take the girls to see the new animated movie," she said, after he'd taken his place on the cushion she'd patted. Then she shrugged. "Will wonders never cease?"

"My grandda always says small miracles are all around. I guess we can count that as one." Then he wondered if there might be any more miracles scheduled for his day where Laurel was concerned. Instead of taking a cookie, he took her hand, thinking the time had come to take the risk. "Did you miss me?" He dipped his head, looking out under his brows and sporting half a smile— his way of acting direct but shy. He hoped she liked it.

Her gaze locked on to his. *Do you want the truth?* those eyes seemed to challenge.

Yes. He. Did. He wanted the truth, and nothing but. He was tired of beating around the bush about their feelings.

"For two whole weeks."

"You did?" You mean he wasn't the only one? A warm, simmering sensation in his chest helped relax his shoulders and boost his outlook. A small miracle?

She slowly nodded, never taking her eyes off him. "I fought with myself, too, because I still wanted to wring your neck for being so reckless. Then I realized my anger was based on lo—caring for you."

They held hands and stared at each other, and Mark wanted to think she'd corrected herself from saying *love*. But caring about someone enough to get that furious had to border on love, didn't it? Whether she said it or not. Because that's how he felt about her. He *loved* her. There was no other way to explain his feelings.

There was something else he needed to know, too. "Have you forgiven me?" He waited a beat, and since she didn't jump right in, he prodded. "Since you came *all the way* over to the hotel with this list? Or do you really just want my fix-it expertise?" he teased, hoping she'd be honest in return.

"I haven't forgiven you, because I'm still working on

forgiving myself for melting down in front of you and my kids and God only knows who else."

"My mother, grandfather…"

She covered her face in shame. "Oh, don't remind me."

His hand flew to her shoulder to comfort her. "It was my fault."

She peeked between her fingers. "You scared the crap out of me."

The leftover fear he saw in her expression made the protective part of him go nuts. All he wanted to do was take her in his arms and promise anything she wanted him to. But this was their chance to lay it all out there, to tell each other how they felt about each other, and decide what to do about it. He couldn't let anything get in the way of that.

"I'm sorry," he said. "You know I am."

"Can you forgive me?"

"For caring about me? Hell, no. That was the first time I realized you might have some feelings for me. Until then I thought we just had a lopsided thing going on where I was falling hard, and you were living in the moment."

His comment seemed to startle her. She narrowed her eyes in disbelief. "I thought you were the one living in the moment and I was the one falling."

Sweet music to his ears. "Now we're getting somewhere, babe. What else haven't you been telling me?" He tugged her to his side, and she rested her head on his shoulder. It felt so great and right to be near her again.

"We had a family meeting about you."

He lifted his chin from the top of her head. "You did? This is really getting good." All that time he'd been moping around they'd held family meetings with him as the topic?

"The kids and I decided we needed you back in our lives."

"The kids and you."

"Uh-huh. Peter said since I'd sent you away, you were being a gentleman, and it was up to me to go to you."

"That Peter is a smart kid."

"Claire and Gracie said I should bring you cookies."

He laughed. "Also smart kids. So I guess I should take one, then." He reached for the freshly baked chocolate cookies and ate one in two bites. Delicious as always, but maybe more so now, with Laurel at his side, and their world opening back up.

She laughed lightly. "The girls also said something in regards to us, and likening it to how Daisy loves Anna and licks her face a lot. I wonder how many times they caught us kissing."

"We did give them a lot of opportunities." He grinned then screwed up his face as it occurred to him. "They thought I was licking you?"

"They're still four, honey."

He especially liked her calling him *honey*.

She went tense again, he felt it in her shoulders. "I'm still not sure I can handle being in a relationship," she continued. "Family meeting or not."

"Who can? But sitting around and waiting for something bad to happen is a waste of time, don't you think?"

"If you put it like that, yes. But I have history, remember?"

"No doubt." He kissed her temple and smoothed her hair. He felt her relax a little. "Look, I can't promise to never get hurt again, or not ever get sick, life is too unpredictable for that. I *can* promise not to take unnecessary risks. But I could be the most cautious guy in the world and step into the street and get hit by a car.

The thing is, we can't control life any more than who we fall in love with." He held her tighter. She'd hinted enough about how she felt about him. Maybe he should tell it straight up, about his feelings. "And speaking of that, I *can* promise one more thing." He sat straight, held her by the shoulders so he could look her in the eyes again. "Because I've given this two full weeks of thought and made changes to my life to prove it. I can promise to love you. Already do. That won't change, whether you love me back or not. It's out of my hands. Too late, babe, I love you. So there."

"I need to catch my breath." Doe-eyed and murmuring, she reached for his face, running her fingers down his cheeks. "I came to ask you back into my life today, because I missed you so, so much. We all did. You're such a good man. Every day I panicked thinking I'd lost you, yet not having the guts to name what I felt." She kissed him softly. "That's another thing I love about you, you don't beat around the bush." Her brows shot up. "You love me? Really?"

"Want me to prove it?"

Her face flushed, her eyes fully dilated. "Yes," she whispered.

He reached for her, then led her back to guest room number three, where he'd just fixed the leaky faucet. They may have tested out the bathtub that day, but they'd never made it to the bed.

"How long is that movie supposed to last?"

Mark hovered above Laurel, ready to enter her. As always, when they made love, he'd worked her into a frenzy by giving every part of her body his utmost attention. He'd already proved beyond a doubt that he loved her. Hell, he'd said the words. Deep in the moment, she wanted him more than anything, but another urgent need made her stop him short of entry. Her hands cupped his face, forcing his wildly sex-charged eyes to delve into hers. His obvious desire jolted through her center, making it hard to speak. But she had to. She hadn't told him yet, and he deserved to know how she felt.

"I love you," she whispered, her body covering with goose bumps as she did.

His smoldering bedroom stare softened with love. They studied each other, isolating the special moment for a time. There was no doubt the feeling was mutual. "You know I love you, too," he said, then with a thrust, they came together. She swore as he moved inside her, it felt different, everything was different, and better than ever. Soon overcome with sensations and reactions thanks to the man she loved, she didn't have any thoughts at all.

Chapter Ten

After Mark and Laurel had finished a lovemaking session hot enough to grill steaks, and topped it off with a long and satisfying shower, Laurel's kids came home. It was a little after four, and she and Mark had started a real barbecue. It occurred to her that they were a couple, whether she was ready for it or not. How could she deny the best thing that'd walked into her life since Alan?

"Burgers coming up," Mark said, as the twins rushed him and hugged his legs.

"We missed you." Gracie was the first to say it, while gazing up at him adoringly. Laurel felt so full of love she didn't know what to do. So she stood and let the goodness run over her, head to toe, and basked in the sweet feeling.

Even Peter's eyes lit up when he saw Mark at the grill, tossing burgers and drinking a canned soda. "Good going, Mom. I guess our plan worked."

She put an arm around her son. "Your plan. You're the man, Peter." They playfully high-fived, and Mark noticed, a smile slanting across his gorgeous face.

"Have you learned how to grill a burger yet, Peter?"

Peter flashed Laurel a help-me glance, but she suspected it was obligatory for being a teenager. She also hoped he not only didn't mind, but looked forward to learning all he could from Mark. If she played it right, maybe he'd get a lifetime of that fatherly attention. Peter leaped down the back porch steps to join his mentor by the fancy grill. "Is this gonna impress girls?"

"Ever met a teenage girl who didn't like hamburgers?"

"Awesome." Her son grinned, and it melted her heart. Though she did worry a little about his wanting to impress girls.

Laurel went back to the kitchen to whip up a salad and check on the sweet potato fries baking in the oven. The golden moment of having her kids *like* the man she'd fallen in love with, after all they'd been through losing their dad, put a grin on her face that started deep inside. After all the years of pain, fear and sadness, they all needed this normal kind of life. For however long it lasted with Mark, she'd decided to give their relationship 100 percent of her effort and attention, because Mark deserved so much. Her mind drifted to earlier that afternoon.

Two weeks later, record waves once again hit the shores all along the central coast. Sandpiper Beach was making history, this time, due to a hurricane down south. Mark, Laurel and the kids couldn't resist taking their beach chairs and setting up for another crazy show. Sweaters on, they watched along with the other lookie-

loos on the crowded beach, while the usual suspects—
wild and fearless surfers—took on the record-breaking
waves.

After his brush with death last month, he wasn't the
least bit tempted to try one out, nor was he envious of
those crazy surfers getting tossed around and battered
by the sea. Still, he and Peter watched with awe as the
surfers seemed brave in battle with the monster waves.

If anyone should be envied it was him. He was a guy
who a few short months ago was as lost as a soul could
be, no plans, no future, no idea how to change his life.
Now he sat with the prettiest gal on the beach and a
ready-made family. A little piece of heaven right there
in Sandpiper Beach.

He'd changed into a guy with potential. Putting the
past behind—though he'd never forget his tours in the
Middle East, or his friends and fellow soldiers who'd
fought so valiantly alongside him, and those who'd been
taken out by IEDs—no, he'd never forget, but he was
finally ready to move on, to quit letting old nightmares
keep him down or hold him back. Today, those memories seemed from a lifetime ago, and he preferred the
here and now. Especially with Laurel in his life. She,
like his parents and brothers, had seen his potential
long before he had. Some days he wondered where he'd
be if he hadn't met and fallen in love with her. Good
thing she'd gotten the crazy idea to buy that old house
and open a B&B.

Surprisingly, he'd enjoyed learning the ins and outs
of the hotel business, and was thankful to his parents for
being patient with him. For the first time in over a year,
he was confident in his knowledge and business sensi-
bilities. Some days he felt ready to take on the world.
With Laurel by his side, why not, he could do anything.

He and Laurel had many conversations about how to grow their businesses, and had come up with some great plans. He'd built the perfect place for weddings, as his mother had the foresight about the gazebo on the large side yard, and Laurel had the ideal honeymoon suite. All the couple had to do was walk across the street. Putting their efforts together, they'd come up with a wedding package approved by his mother, and they'd already booked the first ceremony.

From his seat on the beach, Mark's world, like those wild and crazy waves, was filled with possibilities. His eyes flew open as far in the distance the wave of the century swelled. Everyone saw it and waited, even the kids. So moved by the greatness of Mother Nature, one particular thought came to mind: now was the time. Why not? He looked at Laurel. Like the sandwich that day at her house, her secret sauce still drove him nuts. Always would.

"I have a crazy idea," he said, grinning.

Disbelief widened her eyes, lifted her brows and turned her beautiful smile upside down. "Oh, no, you are not!"

"Oh, yes, I am." He beamed and stood, getting her full attention, though not necessarily in a good way, then dropped to a knee in front of her. "Laurel." He took her hand. "Give me the rest of your life, and I'll prove how much I love you, every single day. Will you marry me?"

That humongous wave must have crashed onto the shore because he could swear the earth moved, and people screamed in awe and clapped behind them. It wasn't because he'd just asked the woman he loved to marry him, that much he knew. All Mark saw was Laurel, with the most amazing expression on her face. A mixture of surprise and love so deep his heart nearly melted.

When the journalists wrote about the record-breaking phenomenon from the sea today, Mark would remember only one thing, which turned out to be far, far greater. His special moment didn't crash onto the shore, or make so much noise everything else got blotted out. His little miracle was a small sound that couldn't even be heard. Fortunately, he could read her lips.

Laurel said yes.

Sunday dinner at the Delaney Pub was crowded and noisy as usual and overflowing with great food, but most importantly, filled with love. Mark had never felt greater in his life. Laurel had said yes to his proposal earlier that afternoon, and now it was time to share their special news with his family.

He waited until everyone was halfway through dinner, when mouths were full and conversations had ebbed. Then he tapped his water glass with his butter knife. *Ting, ting, ting.*

"I have an announcement to make."

Curious eyes rose from around the table, none more so than Grandda's. The room went quiet as forks and cutlery went still. Eyes settled on Mark, and not surprisingly, passing over Laurel first, for a hint. Laurel looking beautiful as always, her hair shining under the pub lights, her eyes bright and dancing with their secret. She smiled demurely and looked to Mark, who sat beside her.

"I've asked Laurel to marry me, and she said yes."

Grandda's palm slammed into the table, in a good way. "I knew it!" He jumped to his feet and danced a little jig. Maureen's hands flew to her cheeks, and Sean grinned until his eyes nearly closed, shaking his head in a will-wonders-ever-cease kind of way. Mark had stepped up to taking over the hotel, hadn't he? Why should his father be surprised about this next step?

Daniel, being recently married himself, was the first to come around the table and slap his brother on the back. "So happy for you." Mark stood so they could hug.

Immediately, they all broke out of their seats, having a total hug fest, everyone hugging everyone else. Congratulations flying left and right.

It had taken a near miracle to keep the proposal private, but thanks to the distraction of a monumental wave, he and Laurel had pulled it off. He'd proposed, she'd said yes, they kissed and the kids thought they were just doing what they always did. Oblivious to the love-you-forever looks walking back to her house, her children didn't have a clue that their world had just changed forever.

Once they were all home, he and Laurel sat the kids in the front parlor and told them their plans. The twins acted like they'd just seen Santa. Peter chewed his lips and sat quietly for a few seconds, then, seeming more like an old man than a teenager said, "I hope you'll be very happy."

Laurel dropped to her knees and hugged her boy until they both cried. "I am happy," she'd said.

"I know, Mom, I can tell."

Then everyone cried and clapped, and the twins jumped up and down until Peter told them to stop it.

In the celebratory chaos, someone tugged on Mark's hand. He looked down. Little Gracie. "Does this mean you'll be my daddy or my pretember daddy?" Evidently, it had taken this long for the question to occur to her.

He bent to meet her face-to-face. "I hope you'll call me Daddy. I want to be."

Peter jumped in. "Dude, are you gonna be like my friend or my father now?" He'd saved up his question, too.

Mark threw an arm around Peter's shoulders. "I hope to be both. Is that okay?"

After giving it some thought, Peter nodded. Mark knew a longer conversation was needed about his role as a step-in dad and that would require Laurel by his side. Together they'd explain to all three of the Prescott kids exactly who he was—a man who loved them with all of his heart—and how he could never replace their real father. He wouldn't ever try to do that. While keeping their father's memory alive, he'd promise to be there for them every day, and they could count on that. But that would have to wait.

Claire pushed her glasses up her nose, standing behind her brother. Mark pulled her closer. "You're okay about me marrying your mom, right?"

"Can I be a flower girl? And wear a princess dress?"

This one never ceased to surprise him. "I don't see why not."

She beamed and threw her arms around his neck. "I'm gonna call you Daddy."

Mark had thought the best part about proposing had happened on the beach when Laurel had said yes. Just now, though, breaking the news to his family and seeing their joy, and then fine-tuning what it all meant with his future kids, came a very close second. But something still nagged at Mark.

Though Conor looked genuinely happy for Mark, he remained on the other side of the table. He'd been instrumental in Mark's regaining his confidence after his breakup from Laurel, but due to Conor's busy schedule, he hadn't been in on all the plans Mark had made. Last Conor knew, Mark was just trying to put the pieces of his life back together by taking on more responsibility with the hotel. The proposal had never been discussed.

Finally, Conor reached across the table to shake Mark's hand. "Congratulations, man. I'm happy for you." There was honest-to-goodness goodwill behind the gesture. Mark felt his sincerity.

"I didn't know I was going to propose to Laurel until I did."

"That's the guy I remember. You were always fearless." Conor's smile widened, and they hugged. His kid brother had remembered all kinds of things Mark had forgotten about himself.

He hoped Conor would find his lucky break, too. He worked hard and kept his nose clean. Plus he still wanted to buy the old Beacham house. Lord only knew what for. He was the kind of guy who needed a special lady who could understand his job, and the way he kept his heart protected since Shelby had broken it. His own special girl had to be out there. Somewhere.

Grandda bear-hugged Mark, breaking his thoughts. "Oh, my boy. Was I right? Huh?"

"Yes, Grandda, you were right. Laurel is a great girl and she's the one for me."

"You know why, don't you." It wasn't a question.

Oh, Lord, there it was, *the look*. And the story behind that look. His engagement to Laurel, in his grandfather's mind, would forever be compliments of a selkie—the seal he and his brothers had saved from orcas eight months back. There would be no arguing the point of fantasy versus reality. So Mark simply accepted it. Yeah, it was the selkie.

Fortunately, Padraig Delaney's attention had now shifted from Mark…to Conor. Poor Conor. Grandda walked to the other side of the long table and cupped the youngest Delaney brother's shoulder. With all the ruckus with Maureen, Keela and Laurel's hugging, laughing and making plans, and the little girls' jumping up and down about getting to wear princess dresses at the wedding, Mark didn't have to hear what his grandfather said to Conor. From across the table Mark read Grandda's lips, then saw Conor's brows shoot halfway up his forehead.

"Lad, you're next," Himself said with complete confidence.

* * * * *

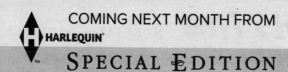

COMING NEXT MONTH FROM

HARLEQUIN®

SPECIAL EDITION

Available April 17, 2018

#2617 THE NANNY'S DOUBLE TROUBLE
The Bravos of Valentine Bay • by Christine Rimmer
Despite their family connection, Keely Ostergard and Daniel Bravo have never gotten along. But when Keely steps in as emergency nanny to Daniel's twin toddlers, she quickly finds herself sweet on the single dad.

#2618 MADDIE FORTUNE'S PERFECT MAN
The Fortunes of Texas: The Rulebreakers
by Nancy Robards Thompson
When Maddie Fortunado's father announces that she and Zach McCarter—Maddie's secret office crush—are competing to be his successor, Maddie's furious. But as they work together to land a high-profile listing, they discover an undeniable chemistry and a connection that might just pull each of them out of the fortifications they've built to protect their hearts.

#2619 A BACHELOR, A BOSS AND A BABY
Conard County: The Next Generation • by Rachel Lee
Diane Finch is fostering her cousin's baby and can't find suitable day care. In steps her boss, Blaine Harrigan, who loves kids and just wants to help. As they grow closer, will the secret Diane is keeping be the thing that tears them apart?

#2620 HER WICKHAM FALLS SEAL
Wickham Falls Weddings • by Rochelle Alers
Teacher Taryn Robinson leaves behind a messy breakup and moves to a small town to become former navy SEAL Aiden Gibson's young daughters' tutor. Little does she know she's found much more than a job—she's found a family!

#2621 THE LIEUTENANTS' ONLINE LOVE
American Heroes • by Caro Carson
Thane Carter and Chloe Michaels are both lieutenants in the same army platoon—and they butt heads constantly. Luckily, they have their online pen pals to vent to. Until Thane finds out the woman he's starting to fall for is none other than the workplace rival he's forbidden to date!

#2622 REUNITED WITH THE SHERIFF
The Delaneys of Sandpiper Beach • by Lynne Marshall
Shelby and Conor promised to meet on the beach two years after the best summer of their lives, but when Shelby never showed, Conor's heart was shattered. Now she's back in Sandpiper Beach and working at his family's hotel. Can Conor let the past go long enough to see if they can finally find forever?

YOU CAN FIND MORE INFORMATION ON UPCOMING HARLEQUIN® TITLES,
FREE EXCERPTS AND MORE AT WWW.HARLEQUIN.COM.

HSECNM0418

But Thane took only one more step before stopping, watching in horror as Michaels entered row D from the other side. Good God, what were the odds? This was ridiculous. It was the biggest night of his life, the night when he was finally going to meet the woman of his dreams, and Michaels was here to make it all difficult.

He retreated. He backed out of the row and went back up a few steps, row E, row F, going upstream against the flow of people. He paused there. He'd let Michaels take her seat, then he'd go back in and be careful not to look toward her end of the row as he took his seat in the center. If he didn't make eye contact, he wouldn't have to acknowledge her existence at all.

He watched Michaels pass seat after seat after seat, smiling and nodding thanks as she worked her way into the row, his horror growing as she got closer and closer to the center of the row, right to where he and Ballerina were going to meet.

No.

Michaels was wearing black, not pink and blue. It was a freak coincidence that she was standing in the center of the row. She'd probably entered from the wrong side and would keep moving to this end, to a seat near his aisle.

The house lights dimmed halfway. Patrons started hustling toward their seats in earnest. Michaels stayed where she was, right in the center, and sat down.

Thane didn't move as the world dropped out from under him.

Then anger propelled him. Thane turned to walk up a few more rows. He didn't want Michaels to see him. He'd wait, out of the way, until he saw Ballerina show up, because Michaels was not, could not be, Ballerina.

He stomped up to row G. Row H.

Not. Possible.

There'd been some mistake. Thane turned around and leaned his back against the wall, leaving room for others to continue past him. He focused fiercely on the row closest to the railing. That was A. The next one back was B, then C, and…D. No mistake. Michaels was sitting in D. In the center.

He glared daggers at the back of her head, hating all those tendrils and curls and flowers. His heart contracted hard in his chest; those flowers in her hair were pink and blue.

Ballerina was Michaels.

Don't miss
THE LIEUTENANTS' ONLINE LOVE by Caro Carson,
available May 2018 wherever
Harlequin® Special Edition books and ebooks are sold.

www.Harlequin.com

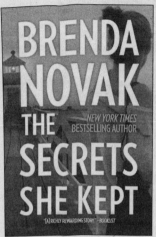

Looking for more satisfying love stories
with community and family at their core?

Check out **Harlequin® Special Edition**
and **Harlequin® Western Romance** books!

New books available every month!

CONNECT WITH US AT:

Harlequin.com/Community

 Facebook.com/HarlequinBooks

 Twitter.com/HarlequinBooks

 Instagram.com/HarlequinBooks

 Pinterest.com/HarlequinBooks

ReaderService.com

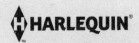

**ROMANCE WHEN
YOU NEED IT**

HFGENRE2017R